I0671910

sex, scandals and sweethearts

In 19th century Boston, a handsome young tutor finds himself the object of more attention than he can comfortably handle. In post-World War Two Japan, a retired serviceman looks back on his forbidden love for a fellow pilot. In Miami, a gay detective pits his wits against a cunning fraudster. And a harassed career woman discovers that all manner of mishaps can befall you if you neglect to brush your teeth...

This collection of 18 short stories, by turns humorous, poignant and chilling, explores the lives and loves of an unforgettable cast of characters as they search for acceptance in a world that doesn't always understand them.

Published by
NineStar Press
PO Box 91792
Albuquerque, New Mexico, 87199
www.ninestarpress.com

Warning: This book contains scenes of graphic violence and sexually explicit content which is only suitable for mature readers.

Print ISBN # 978-1-911153-87-0
Original Cover Art by Aria Tan
Print Cover by Natasha Snow
Edited by Elizabeth Coldwell

GOTTA DANCE WITH THE ONE WHO BRUNG YA

sex, scandals, and sweethearts

A Short Story Collection

Jon McDonald

Dedication

To Sheri who gets it.

Acknowledgements

These stories were first published in the following publications:

Cheap Trick in the Drunk Tank, *Jonathan*

Dangling Participles and Fly Boys, *Laurel Online*

Midnight Clear, *Santa Fe New Mexican*

Cry of the Wolf, *ImageOutWrite 2012*

You Are a Winner! *Off the Rocks, Vol. 17*

Fly Boys, *Off the Rocks, Vol. 19*

Table of Contents

Dangling Participles

To say that Dexter Wiggin was handsome would be a gross understatement. He was radiant. He had the fair skin of a maiden. His midnight-black hair set off his fine features in sharp contrast. Whether in profile or full face, his perfect head graced a slim, supple body equally admired. But oh, how he suffered. He was *so* extremely shy and retiring as to be almost pathological. Growing up with no siblings in the small town of Quincy, south of Boston, he had lived quietly with his mother—his father having been killed in the Civil War at Appomattox. He was bright, studious, and sang like an angel in the church choir. He was often teased by the other boys because of his stunning, androgynous looks, which drove him even deeper within himself. The headmaster at his school sought to guide him into law, thinking he would make a fine attorney with his sharp mind, but Dexter was far too modest and timid to take up that profession. And, of course, the military was totally out of the question for a young man of his sensitivity.

Instead, after graduating from Harvard at twenty-three, he took the position of tutor with a prominent Boston family—the Howlands. He was engaged to lead the studies of the twins, shy eighteen-year-old Charles, and his sister, Flora—a ravishing beauty who was completely full of herself.

Trevor Howland and his wife, Martha, who were often engaged in social and civic duties, seldom had time to monitor their children and were greatly relieved to finally have a fine young gentleman with a sterling reputation in charge of the moral and scholarly education of their somewhat rambunctious progeny.

Dexter could see that he had his work cut out for him, though, especially with Flora. She already considered herself a grown woman and had little use for the distractions of any further education—even

1

though her mother insisted she master French, as it was considered such a fine, ladylike accomplishment in Boston social circles.

Flora was slouched at the breakfast table and had a ribbon in her hand that she was winding around her forefinger. She would not look up at Dexter even when he spoke to her.

"Flora, have you studied the verbs I assigned you yesterday?"

Flora pouted and pulled the ribbon off her finger in one grand gesture, flinging it out toward Dexter with a snap like a whip. "Nasty old French verbs. I hate them." She rose from the table and flounced out of the room, totally ignoring Dexter's entreaties for her to remain.

Poor Dexter hated confrontation of any kind. And despite the authority granted him by the Howlands, he had absolutely no will to exercise his disciplinary prerogatives with Flora at the moment.

But at least there was Master Charles, a somewhat sheltered and naïve but willing student, and an eager, wide-eyed acolyte. He hung on Dexter's every word and ferociously completed every assignment with great enthusiasm and mastery. This afternoon, however, Master Charles seemed to be having a hard time concentrating on his English grammar assignment. The schoolroom window was open for the first time this spring, and Charles was gazing outside at the maple tree putting out its first few tentative leaves. A soft warm breeze played with the curtains at the window. And he was further distracted by the sounds of the horses and carriages in the street outside. It appeared poor Charles could not get his mind around to the subject at hand.

"Please, read me your last sentence," Dexter demanded of Charles once again.

"What?" Charles snapped back into the present. He looked down at his exercise book. "Ah, ah..." He read again the sentence he had just finished. "Rushing to finish his essay, Tom's pencil broke."

"Now, tell me what's wrong with that sentence," Dexter quizzed.

Charles stared blankly at the notebook. He shrugged. "I've no idea, sir."

"You have a dangling participle. The verb and the subject do not agree. 'Rushing'—the participle and verb—does not agree with the noun: 'pencil'. The pencil is not rushing, Tom is. Thus the participle—rushing—

is dangling."

Charles stared up at Dexter in complete bewilderment.

"Now complete the sentence so that it makes sense, please," Dexter demanded.

Dexter was standing in front of the open window. He was backlit and, as he turned his head toward Charles, the sun broke through the clouds for a brief moment and lit up Dexter's face like the subject of the Dutch painting in the library. Charles was stunned. It was a defining and illuminating moment in his life. He had never seen anything so absolutely beautiful before. He felt stirrings in his loins that he could not account for, and he rushed out of the classroom. "Excuse me, Mr. Wiggin, I have to leave the room."

When Charles returned, he appeared flushed. He had obviously splashed water on his face, as his hair was slightly wet. He stood in the doorway, not sure how he should proceed.

"Are you coming in, Master Charles?" Dexter queried.

"Sir. Sir," was all he could muster in response.

"What is it, Charles, are you ill?"

"Sir..." Charles suddenly rushed forward to where Dexter was now sitting at his desk. He took Dexter's hand in both of his. "Sir." He leaned forward and kissed the back of Dexter's hand with great intensity. He abruptly straightened, letting go of Dexter's hand, stared at him like a startled deer, and then turned and rushed out of the room.

The soft breeze blew a curtain against the back of Dexter's neck. He lightly brushed it away. He was utterly bewildered, and uncertain now as to how he should respond. Should he go after his charge, or pretend it never happened? Paralyzed with indecision, he was blushing brightly, and for the first time felt he might not be up to the task of tutoring this household. He was frantic with regret and guilt, even though he had instigated nothing. He was far too embarrassed to speak to Charles directly and could only think to retire to his attic room, lie down, and restore his equilibrium.

He rushed out of the schoolroom and headed for the main staircase leading to his room. But as he passed by the solarium, Madam's voice called out to him.

"Oh Mr. Wiggin, may I see you for a moment, please?"

Dexter froze in the dash to his chambers. He was certain that Charles had told his mother everything, and he would now be tossed out of the house in utter disgrace and humiliation—even though he had done nothing.

"Madam," he responded, and hesitantly poked his head through the solarium doorway.

"Please come in, won't you?" Madam smiled and patted a welcoming place on the sofa next to where she was seated with a tea tray on the table in front of her. "Tea?" she offered with a smile as she began to pour even before he consented.

Dexter was beginning to feel that perhaps Charles had not communicated the unfortunate occurrence to his mother after all.

"Tea would be nice." He sat gingerly on the edge of the sofa, a comfortable distance away from Madam.

"Milk, sugar, lemon?" she asked, the cup poised in her hand.

"Lemon only, thank you."

Madam placed a small slice of lemon on his saucer with a pair of silver tongs.

"Do have a lemon tart. It will be such a delicious compliment to your tea." And again, without his response, she placed a small yellow nugget of tart on a plate and handed both the tea and the tart to Dexter.

It was late afternoon now and the sun was spilling into the garden room with the force of the burgeoning spring. Mr. Howland was quite fond of orchids, and the mossy, woody haze of the solarium air was set in motion by the afternoon sun streaming in through the double glazed windows. Dexter was beginning to feel uncomfortable. He was not used to sweating, and he delicately brushed back a lock of hair off his now moist brow. Madam remained as cool as the cucumber sandwich, *sans* crusts, on which she was ever so politely nibbling. Her blonde curls were as perfect as an alabaster frieze. Her muslin dress was taut and trim across her breasts and around her perfect little waist.

"More tea, Mr. Wiggin?" She slightly lowered her gaze and turned more directly to him.

"Thank you, no." He was even more uncomfortable now. Madam

did not seem to have a perceptible reason for calling him into the garden room. The scent of the orchids was becoming cloying, and he felt that he might soon fall into a swoon if he did not escape this oppressive atmosphere. He put down his teacup.

"I really feel I must get back to my room now." He spoke abruptly. "I have to prepare the lessons for tomorrow's classes."

"Oh please don't go just yet, Mr. Wiggin. It has been such a pleasure sharing afternoon tea with you." She reached over and placed her hand on Dexter's knee. He was so startled he actually executed a slight jump on the sofa. He looked around wildly. The giant ferns seemed to imprison him. The philodendron, climbing the pillars, scowled down on him—ancient, disapproving gargoyles. The scarlet hibiscus scolded from their pots in the corners of the room.

Madam gave a crystalline laugh and scooted closer, placing her arm lightly around Dexter's shoulders as her other hand slid slowly up his leg. "Now Mr. Wiggin, I got the impression in our first meeting that you were a man of the world. I certainly wasn't wrong, was I? A Harvard man, after all," she uttered, as Dexter strove to disentangle himself from her advances.

"Madam," he asserted as he rose from the sofa and backed toward the entrance, "I'm afraid you must have a mistaken idea about me. I am your family tutor, and I have a responsibility that does not allow for familiarities with *any* members of the family. I am gravely sorry if you have found me wanting."

Again Madam laughed lightly and leaned back against the sofa, her arm languishing along the back. "Oh Mr. Wiggin. Are you always so serious? My, my. Do come back." She patted the sofa seat next to her. He refused to move. "Well, you have quite bewitched me, what can I say? Surely you don't want to fall into my bad graces now, do you?" And then, with just an edge of pleading, "Dexter, certainly the life of a solitary bachelor cannot be long endured—a handsome, virile, young man of your age. I'm certain you must have needs as well. Just imagine how advantageous it could be to both of us if you could melt just a little." She scooted along the sofa even closer toward Dexter.

Just then, Charles came bounding into the garden room. He froze and blushed bright pink upon seeing Dexter with his mother. He feared the worst. It was all over now. Mr. Wiggin had certainly revealed all about his schoolroom indiscretion.

Madam looked intently at Charles. "My dear, do come closer. You look so flushed. Do you have a fever?"

Charles sidled over to his mother, who put her hand up to his forehead. He kept his eyes on Mr. Wiggin and awaited the reproach from Mama. But none came. She pulled him around so he faced her square on.

"I think some hot water and lemon and then to bed for the rest of the afternoon. Don't you think, Mr. Wiggin?"

"It might be advisable."

"No, I'm fine, Mother—really," Charles pleaded, wanting only to escape the solarium at this moment.

"Now don't argue with your mother, Charles. Mr. Wiggin, would you please kindly escort Master Charles to his bedroom, and see that he gets undressed immediately and put into bed. I shall have Clara bring up the hot water and lemon straight away."

Poor Charles was now doubly confounded—not only was there the kiss earlier, but now he must completely undress and stand naked in front of Mr. Wiggin. He was not at all sure what the result of *that* might be.

Dexter was also feeling uncomfortable about this development for much the same reason.

"I'm not quite sure that Master Charles needs my assistance, Madam. At eighteen and with his agile mind, I am certain that he can undress and get himself into bed quite efficiently without my supervision."

Madam paused, brushed a crumb from her dress, and turned to Mr. Wiggin once again. "I seem to remember, Mr. Wiggin, that in our interview with you for this position, you clearly stated that you would be *more* than willing—nay, eager even—to assist any member of our family with *any* need that might arise. So far I have not witnessed that willingness, Mr. Wiggin. Am I to assume that you no longer desire to continue in this position?" She smiled very sweetly.

"I am very much obliged to assist Master Charles, as you wish, of course."

"And as to the other matter that we were discussing earlier, I shall wish to resume our conversation on that subject again at another time—soon. Good afternoon." She waved the two away and sank back into the sofa where a delicate ghost orchid seemed to whisper in her ear.

Dexter marched Charles to his room. Neither of them spoke about the kiss, but Charles was clearly nervous and expecting a reprimand. Dexter, however, could not muster such a response and quickly left the room as soon as Charles had undressed himself and slipped into bed, gratefully, without any further incidents.

Dexter was so distraught after the episodes with Madam and Charles that he went directly to his room. He asked that his dinner be sent up to his chambers that evening, and retired early with the idea that a good night's sleep would refresh him and allow him to more fully consider the consequences of what was happening in this wretched house.

☆ ☆ ☆

It was about one in the morning. Dexter knew because he had just turned over in bed, surfacing slightly from sleep, and heard the church bell chime the hour. It was then that he became aware of the very slightest movement in his room—a rustling. He was instantly awake and sat up in bed and peered into the darkness. There at his door was a faint white shape.

"Hello?" he called out.

The shape moved hesitantly forward but stopped, still some distance from his bed. He was unable to make out who it was.

"Who's there? What do you want?"

Suddenly the form rushed forward, and Flora threw herself on top of Dexter, flinging him back onto his bed.

"Oh Dexter, my beloved, I can resist you no longer."

Dexter tried freeing himself from her, but she was straddling him, and her hands were holding down his arms in a vise-like grip.

"Flora, please get off. This is totally inappropriate."

"Oh my darling, do you not feel the same about me? I have lain awake many nights thinking only of you."

She leaned down and gave him a moist, passionate kiss. He turned his head away and struggled to free himself from her grasp. She reached down and slid her hand under his nightshirt. But by releasing one of his hands to do this, it allowed Dexter to finally get some leverage, and he pushed on the bed with great force and flung the quite distraught Flora most ungraciously onto the floor. Dexter immediately lit the lamp by his bed, pulled down his nightshirt, and put on a robe.

"I don't know what to say to you, Flora."

Flora rose from the floor and rushed forward, flinging her arms around Dexter's neck.

"I can't help myself. I am consumed with love for you," she sighed.

As Dexter was considerably taller than Flora, she could not quite reach up to kiss him again, as he was leaning backward, trying to pull away from her. So she threw her arms tightly around Dexter's torso, buried her head in his chest, and began to cry.

Once again, Dexter was utterly perplexed. What was it about this family? Yes, he had been admired all his life for his stunning looks. But never before had he been so unrelentingly accosted. He finally managed to pry Flora from him and held her out at arm's length.

"Flora, this has got to stop, right now. I will not tolerate this. You have somehow turned my concern for you as your tutor into some kind of romantic nonsense. Let me assure you that I have absolutely *no* romantic interest in you whatsoever."

At that, Flora gave a soul-wrenching cry and fled the room as quickly as she could. Poor Dexter collapsed onto the edge of his bed and rested his head in his hands. It was clear to him now that this was a *very* disturbed family, and he decided that he would have to give his notice to Mr. Howland first thing in the morning. Needless to say, he did not get much sleep the rest of the night.

☆☆☆

Mr. Howland was in his study first thing in the morning, and Dexter was determined not to delay tendering his resignation. What he had

8

wrestled with all night was how to do this without incriminating the rest of the family. It would be entirely inappropriate for Dexter to disclose to the head of the family the indiscretions of his wife and two children.

"Sir, might I have a word with you?" Mr. Howland looked up from his paper and nodded. "I regret having to do this, sir, but I have had word that my mother is gravely ill, and I must return home."

"Indeed? I am saddened to hear that."

"And as I don't know what the situation is with her, or how long I might have to remain in Quincy, I believe it best if I tender my resignation now."

Mr. Howland was silent as he contemplated this news. He put down the newspaper and, rising, crossed over to his desk. He turned and looked out the window at the blustery spring morning.

"Sir?" Dexter was becoming unsettled by the long silence.

Mr. Howland turned to face Dexter. "Son, I don't believe a word you're saying." He walked over, put his arm around Dexter's shoulder, and led him to the window.

"But sir...sir," Dexter stammered.

"No, no, listen. I don't care what you told me. You mother may be ill or not, but I know that's not the issue. I've taken quite a liking to you, my boy, and I know my children are devoted to you as well, even after such a short period of time. If it's a matter of money..."

"No, sir, it's not that."

"Well, it must be something else, then." He paused and turned to look directly at Dexter. "Is it my wife?" Dexter turned pale and looked away. "She and I lead very separate lives, except for the family, of course. She's a very attractive woman and has a great many admirers. And she is not above entertaining them, if you know what I mean. I am guessing she expressed an interest in you that has not been reciprocated." He paused and looked directly at Dexter.

"Sir, I cannot say." Dexter was now extremely uncomfortable and moved away from Mr. Howland.

"Well, I'm guessing you might not follow that particular persuasion. Am I correct?" He walked over to Dexter and put his arm around Dexter's shoulder once again. "As I've said, I've taken quite a liking to

9

you, and I feel that we might have a lot in common, you and me. If you could find your way to accommodate me, then I am certain you would benefit greatly. I have a great many friends who could offer you similar companionship; they are highly placed gentlemen, all with sterling connections for the advancement of a young man of your persuasion. And I am certain we could offer you a far more generous salary for your position here at this house. What do you say?"

Dexter was now in utter panic and could not even speak. He just looked incredulously at Mr. Howland and fled the study. He rushed up the stairs to his room, threw his few belongings into his bag, and fled the house without saying good-bye to anyone. He went directly to the stables where his horse was quartered and searched for Daniel, the groom.

"Daniel, you there?" Dexter called out.

"Sir?" Daniel responded, emerging from his small room behind the stable. "Were you wanting something, sir?"

"Yes, my horse, as soon as possible. I am leaving."

"Going for a ride, sir?"

"No, I'm leaving this house and all its degenerate occupants."

"Sir?" Daniel queried, somewhat confused.

"I've resigned my post. I'm going home."

"Oh that is a pity, it is, a handsome young gentleman like yourself. Why, I was thinking that you and I might go riding together one day. I know some really beautiful spots where there are no prying eyes—if you get my meaning, sir."

Dexter stared at Daniel in utter disbelief. "No, not you too?"

Dexter sat with his mother by their fireplace with its warm and comforting fire. It was still nippy, even this late into the spring.

"I don't know. I just don't know," Dexter responded to his mother's question about what he was going to do next.

"Well, Mr. Todd, I hear, is looking for a tutor for his six children. All sorts of ages. From six to about sixteen, I believe. You should stop by and have a chat with the Mistress. I'm sure they would find you most agreeable."

"Yes, I'm sure they would. But no thank you, Mother, no more tutoring for me."

"Really? Well, you must have had a very nasty experience up there in Boston, then. Why won't you tell me about it? You've been so secretive ever since you've been back home. What happened? Do tell me, dear."

"No, Mother, I don't think I can." He paused and was lost in contemplation for a moment. Then he looked up at her. "But I have reached a decision. I'm going to become a priest. I crave a totally spiritual life. I'll go into the seminary, where there are all those young men just like me—so chaste, so pure. It will be the perfect place for me, don't you see? And then, finally, I shall have some peace."

MoonDrops

MoonDrops: A soothing and sensual blend of nature's own organic, wild-crafted, essential oils, designed to create the ultimate experience of pampered luxury at an affordable price. Within our wide selection of premium blends, you will certainly find many combinations to meet your most discriminating needs and desires. Let your imagination soar as you browse the tantalizing selection of our quality products. Remember, there are no limits to your imagination, and no restrictions to our unconditional guarantee of purity, performance or pleasure.

Sharon McAllister leaned back into her chair and re-read what she had just written on the computer. She was putting together pages for her new website. Up until now, she had been a modest, homegrown operation, housed out of a shed at the back of the house where she concocted her blends of oils from wild-crafted flowers, roots, and stems.

She would collect the orders from her post office box, process them, and make a trip once or twice a week back into Chama to mail out her collection of parcels, fulfilling her few orders.

She had been running a small classified ad in a couple of health food and New Age magazines, and she had managed to make a few bucks along the way. But her brother had been urging her to go to the next level with her business. He was a very successful IT consultant who ran his business from home and knew all about Internet businesses. He knew a website would boost her sales, and he had offered to put the website together for her when he visited from Los Angeles. He would be arriving later this afternoon.

Chama, New Mexico was in the middle of God's own nowhere, way up by the Colorado border where the nearest airport was Albuquerque

13

(for any decent flights)—a good three hours away in fair weather. Sharon would have to be climbing into the pickup and heading out in the next twenty minutes.

She was pleased with what she had written so far. She shut down the computer and went to her bedroom. She still had to dress, but first she sat at her dressing table and brushed out her long mane of auburn hair one hundred times. She had done this ever since she was a little girl under her mother's tutelage. She never missed doing this, and as a result, her hair was lustrous and supple. She put a few drops of Hair Wonder, one of her essential oil blends, on her hands and ran them through her hair. She cocked her head as she gazed into the mirror and thought she looked quite a bit younger than her fifty-plus years. Maybe a few pounds overweight, but that came with age and genetics, and not inactivity on her part. She rose from her dressing table and dressed, as it was time to head out.

☆☆☆

Sharon pulled up to the passenger arrival zone at the Albuquerque International Airport. Daniel was already waiting for her at the curb, and he threw his bag into the back of the pickup and climbed into the passenger seat. He leaned over and gave Sharon a kiss on the cheek.

"Hi, Sis," he offered as he settled in for the drive back to Chama.

"You hungry? Shall we stop for a bite?" Sharon asked.

"Nah, I'm fine. The plane was a little early getting in, and I grabbed a sandwich before you came." He turned to her. "Unless *you* need to stop."

She shook her head. "I'm really glad you decided to visit. I've been worrying about you." She glanced over at Daniel.

Daniel nodded but didn't answer.

"I'm sorry I couldn't make it to the funeral, Danny. I just couldn't get away. There was nobody to watch the animals."

"Yeah. I know." But he didn't sound too convinced.

"I'm sorry I never got to meet Hartley. You guys were always welcome to visit."

"We almost did, once. Hartley had a weekend business conference in Santa Fe, and we both came. But we just didn't have enough time to drive all the way up to Chama. But we did call you, remember?"

"Oh yeah. When was that? 'Bout three years ago?"

Daniel smiled. "He would have liked you. He always had a thing for brassy broads. He always wanted to be Auntie Mame." They both laughed.

"Did he suffer a lot?" she asked.

"Cancer of the esophagus is tough to swallow."

Sharon was taken aback by the crassness of the remark and looked over at Daniel.

"It's okay. It's a little joke. Not in the best taste, huh? But that was Hartley's way of dealing with it. He never took himself too seriously. Even with the cancer."

"Yeah, I would have liked him too," Sharon added.

Daniel was quite unlike Sharon. He was slight, even at thirty-two. He had jet-black hair like his father. Sharon took after her mother. He always joked that he was a mistake as he came so late in his parents' lives. Both parents were now deceased, and it was only Sharon who had been willing to stay and take over the family farm. But there was no resentment on her part toward her brother because he had fled their sleepy little town. She was a natural to keep the farm going and had developed her interest in essential oils, turning it into a modest hobby if not yet a thriving business.

Sharon looked over at Danny and took his hand. "I'm really glad you decided to visit. I know it's been difficult for you to come back. I can't imagine our little backwater was much of a challenge for a bright gay kid like you growing up."

Daniel looked at her. "Yeah, well, let's not dwell on that, okay? Gotta let that kid stuff go, or it drives you crazy."

Sharon patted his hand. "Glad to hear that."

"So, have you been putting some ideas together for the website?" Daniel tactfully changed the subject.

"I have. Done ya proud, kid. Just you wait and see," she joked.

"Gotta get you makin' some real money. Chickens, sheep, goats, and beets won't cut it for long," he teased.

Sharon turned serious again. "Danny, I hope you'll take some time while you're here to grieve a little for Hartley. I've got some really nice oils that will help you work through your process."

Danny didn't respond.

It was almost midnight by the time the truck bounced up the dirt road to the farm.

Danny yanked his bag out of the back of the truck. They went into the house, entering through the kitchen, which had a warm and cozy glow from the lamp hanging over the beat-up kitchen table where so many meals had been shared by the McAllister family.

"Really glad you're here." Sharon pulled Danny to her and looked deeply into his eyes. "Just a moment." She went to the windowsill over the sink and rummaged through some tiny bottles. She came back with two. "Here." She proceeded to rub some oil from the first bottle into Danny's temples. "Life Lessons, this one's called." She opened a second—Grief Relief. "There." She massaged some of this oil into his third eye. She stood back and looked at him again. "Better? Want some soup?"

"I'm exhausted. Think I'll just head straight to bed if you don't mind. But thanks anyway."

"I gotta work on the garden tomorrow. Been neglecting it a bit. Maybe you could help me with some watering." She smiled, knowing he could not refuse her.

"Sure."

Daniel went to his old room. Sharon lingered in the kitchen, heating up some cream of broccoli soup and making a cup of chamomile tea.

☆☆☆

Daniel felt like Danny, the kid he had been, as he sat on the edge of the single bed in his darkened childhood room, staring out the window. A full moon flooded his old desk by the window. He had overcome his many childhood disappointments—or so he thought. Now the room seemed to swirl with memories and hauntings from his past.

Danny had never been perceived as a fag in school. He was not one of those poor kids who were hounded mercilessly because of the way

16

they looked, or walked, or talked. He was tall for his age and manly from hard work on the farm. And though he did not play sports—which he loathed—he excelled at academics and was the leader in many clubs. He even considered running for class president once but finally declined as he perceived it as being beneath him.

Danny had put himself on a pedestal. He had a heroic vision of himself. He was the ultimate white knight—a defender of maidenhood, a holder of primal truths, a paragon of moral virtue—Lancelot before Guinevere. He neither smoked nor drank. He eschewed drugs of any kind, even refusing aspirin for a headache. He belonged to a select group of kids from some of the 'better' families who hung out together, dating within the group, and who pretty much ruled the non-jock side of school. Daniel was great at math and English. He was on the yearbook and head of the debate team. He dated Susanna Calderon from the group—a girl from one of the leading northern New Mexico families, who was a strict Catholic girl. She was as chaste and pure as a hothouse flower—an orchid without scent. This suited Daniel to a T, as it provided him cover for never having to have sex with her. But he could not admit this to himself—just yet.

But as successful as Danny was at projecting his white knight image, he suspected that he might be, indeed, different. There was a structural flaw in his perfect alabaster persona. And it finally cracked and came crashing down in the summer he turned eighteen, between his junior and senior years.

Randal 'Randy' Miller was six years older than Daniel. He worked for the Cumbres and Toltec Scenic Railway as a brakeman. He was a friend of Sharon's and would stop by the farm now and then to pick up fresh eggs for his family—a wife and twin girls. Every time he visited, when Danny was around, Danny would find an excuse to hang out at the chicken barn as Sharon collected eggs for Randy.

Randy had a shock of coarse blond hair that stuck up from his head like a rumpled haystack. It was never combed. He had twinkling blue eyes the color of robin's eggs. And his laugh was infections and his smile disarming. Danny was a total wreck each time Randy drove away in his truck with a wave and a chaotic smile.

One Saturday afternoon when Danny was in town at the supermarket doing some errands for his mom, Randy came over as Danny was putting the groceries in the truck.

"Hey there, big guy." Randy beamed.

Danny was stunned by how totally flustered he was by such a simple greeting.

"Hey," was all he could muster in response.

Randy stared at him for a long minute without speaking. Then he asked, "You ever been to the rail yard?"

Danny shook his head—still unable to find his voice.

"I see." Randy's eyes seemed to bore into the very essence of Danny's being—he was stripped naked and totally exposed.

"How'd you like to go over to the yards with me? Love to show you around. Got a new vintage carriage in. Been stripping it down and fixin' it up to go on line next summer. How about it? Got time?"

Danny's heart was racing. "Yeah. Sure."

Danny was both exhilarated and terrified. Could it be? Was this about something *more* than just a tour of the facilities? Oh yes, it was. And this became the day that Danny McAllister finally climbed down off his pedestal. Today, Little Danny McAllister officially became a full blown, unadulterated, and card-carrying H-O-M-O-S-E-X-U-A-L.

What happened in the railway carriage *that* day was still dear to Danny's heart to *this* day, and he smiled as he sat on the edge of his bed in the dark.

He and Randy carried on their secret affair until Danny went away on scholarship to Stanford University a year and a half later. Danny had some mild concerns that Randy had a wife he was cheating on, but with an eighteen-year-old's hormones, he wasn't *that* concerned.

Needless to say, Danny's life began to change at school. He started growing out his hair. He dumped poor Susanna Calderon faster than an archbishop hiding his mistress when the cardinal came a-calling. And he began to hang out with the semi-demimonde of the school and local artistic communities. He even ventured into his first gay bar in Durango with his fake ID one weekend when he was supposed to be visiting a sick friend. Uh huh.

Daniel finally lay back on his bed. He'd had quite enough of rummaging through the closet of his closeted past. He just wanted to rest. Hartley flashed briefly in his mind just before he fell asleep and the moon washed over him, the river Lethe carrying him swiftly into deep slumber—the succulent scents of Sharon's application of MoonDrops wafting through his dreams.

☆☆☆

Sharon had risen early, as usual, the next morning. She made fresh coffee and left it out for Daniel along with an assortment of breakfast treats. She had fed the chickens, tended to the sheep and goats, checked her herb drying racks, hoed the row of beans, and was now in her shed bottling her new line—Mystical Memories, a memory enhancement product.

She heard the creak of the shed door.

"Danny, did you get some breakfast?" she asked, totally engrossed in her bottling.

She almost spilled the bottle she was gently pouring into a funnel when she was grabbed from behind and had a kiss planted on the side of her neck. She gasped and turned to find herself in Randy's arms. He was beaming—a teasing smile flashed.

"Oh, how you startled me," Sharon scolded as she disengaged herself from Randy's hug. He laughed, turning her around and grabbing her again, this time planting a big, wet kiss on her cheek. "Don't think you can just sweep me off my feet anytime you please, mister." She laughed, just loving the attention. "Here." She applied a touch of the oil she had been pouring to the end of Randy's nose. "Maybe this will help you remember to call me before you just show up," she teased.

She heard the shed door open again, and she could see Danny over Randy's shoulder, his mouth hanging open in wide-eyed disbelief. He backed up as Sharon disengaged herself from Randy's hug. Randy turned and saw Daniel.

"Hey buddy, how's it going?" Randy sailed over to Daniel, his hand extended for a handshake. "You sure are looking mighty good there, fella."

Daniel didn't respond to the offered hand, but seemed to freeze. Randy threw his arms around Daniel in a big hug. Daniel shot a look at Sharon, pleading for an explanation.

Randy pulled back from the hug and looked straight into Daniel's eyes. "Hey, you are one sharp-lookin' dude. Where the hell you been keepin' yourself? How come you never visit?"

"LA," Daniel finally answered. "I live there now."

Sharon came over and put a hand on Randy's shoulder. "Danny just lost his partner to cancer. He's up for a family visit."

Randy's smile quickly faded. "Oh hey, I'm sorry, man. Didn't know."

"Yeah." Danny backed away and immediately left the shed. He hurried back toward the house. But Randy sprinted after him, catching up with him just before Danny went inside. He grabbed Danny and turned him around.

"I'm so sorry," Randy said, holding Danny to him.

Danny pulled fiercely away. "What the fuck!" he shouted as he backed away from Randy.

Randy was shocked. He took a step backward.

"*You* and my *sister*?" Daniel's indignation was raw.

"Hey, hey. It's alright," Randy pleaded, reaching his arms out toward Daniel. "You know, we're really great friends."

"Friends! It sure looked like a lot more than friends just now."

"Well, we see each other now and then. You know how it is."

"You got a wife and two girls..."

"Got a boy now too..."

"A wife and three kids...And you played around with me for a year and a half...and now my sister?"

"Well hey—a guy's got needs..." Randy managed a charming smile.

Daniel stood looking at Randy, shaking his head and wondering what he ever saw in this guy. Then a ray of sun cut through a cloud, illuminating Randy in a golden glow—his ragged hair a boyish tousle, his iceberg-melting, crooked smile flickering—and Danny remembered why.

☆☆☆

Daniel stood at the top of Sharon's vegetable garden with the hose. He was running the water between the rows, letting it soak deep into the roots. As he moved from row to row, tears were streaming down his cheeks. Sharon was raking up in the chicken pen when she looked over and saw Daniel crying.

She went over to him. "Hey, sweetie, you okay?"

"Oh yeah." He started laughing as he wiped the tears away. "I was just thinking about Hartley. He so loved his roses, and this watering reminded me of him getting out of bed in the morning and going outside to water while it was still cool so the water wouldn't burn the buds. He would stand there—stark naked—singing Maria Callas arias at the top of his voice. Said they were diva roses and needed the appropriate stimulation. Fortunately, we had a walled garden or the neighbors would have had such a treat."

Sharon laughed and gave Danny a hug. "How old was he?"

"Can you believe he was only thirty-five?" He paused and gave a sad smile. "Never thought it would end like that. We were even planning to adopt a couple of kids. You know, the kind nobody else wanted—outcasts like us."

Daniel had finished the watering, and he and Sharon dragged the hose back to the shed.

Daniel had never spoken to Sharon about his past with Randy. He didn't think she knew about that, and he didn't want to upset her if she was having a happy little affair with the scalawag now. He had come to the farm to get away from LA for a while, and to get a little TLC from Sharon. And now here he was, wanting to protect and nourish her—knowing that, one day, Randy would surely disappoint her and let her down as well.

Daniel gratefully realized that he was, indeed, healing. His good cry over Hartley had cleansed his soul, and he was feeling lighter, able to see his own life with more clarity and purpose. He was ready to move on.

He put his arm around Sharon. "You ready to put that website together now?"

"You bet."

"Great, then show me what you got."

☆☆☆

They labored the rest of the day on the computer, and by late afternoon, both were exhausted but happy with the results. Danny assured Sharon her business would grow and advised her on how she should handle the additional orders.

Danny felt a celebration was in order and offered to go into town to shop for a really delicious dinner he wanted to make for her, as he was an excellent cook. She was happy to have him make the dinner and gave him the keys to the truck.

As Daniel drove into town, he began to think about life after Hartley. He wanted to clean out all the closets and paint the bedroom the Tuscan yellow that Hartley hated. He became excited about knocking out the window overlooking the garden and putting in French doors and a flagstone patio, where he could breakfast with the two dogs and read the morning paper till noon if he so desired.

Daniel felt just a twinge of anxiety and excitement as he neared the turnoff to the road that led to Randy's fishing cabin. This is where he and Randy would go after school to "make out", as Randy so euphemistically characterized their hot and heavy sex sessions. But there was also a faint smile on Daniel's face as he recalled their activities.

As he was nearing the turnoff, he saw Randy's truck pull out onto the road just ahead of him. Randy did not see him, but Daniel certainly saw the young man in the passenger seat—young and fresh as a ripe peach. Daniel knew all too well where they had been, and what they had been up to. He followed behind—just far enough away so as to not be in danger of being recognized by Randy.

Randy drove to a residential street and let the boy out of the truck, certainly several houses away from the boy's home. Daniel was more than familiar with the routine. Randy drove away, and Daniel again followed.

Randy pulled up to a gas station and began to fill his truck. Daniel parked and walked over.

Randy looked up and saw Daniel approaching.

"Hey there, bud. How's tricks?" Randy beamed, in his ever so winning way.

"I don't know. Not much into tricks these days. But I see you still are."

"What?" Randy suddenly became nervous.

"How's the fishing?" Daniel sneered. Randy was silent. "Saw you coming from the cabin. Same one we used to visit of an afternoon. Cute kid. Was he just cutting your grass?"

Randy gave a strained laugh. "Well, he's eighteen, you know—totally legal. Hey—you know how it is."

"Yeah, I do. And what exactly am I going to tell Sharon? Does she know about your school age extracurricular activities?"

"Now Danny, no need to go and shake the tree. She and I are cool with things as they are. She knows I'm married and all. She knows I like to play. Just leave it alone, will ya? For old time's sake. Okay?"

Daniel just stared and shook his head. "Boy, getting back to Los Angeles is going to be such a relief. These small town melodramas just wear me out."

Randy finished filling his tank, and as he put the hose back on the pump said, "I'm not due back at the house for a while. Want to come back to the fishing shack with me for a little rerun?"

Daniel caught his breath, shook his head, and wondered what MoonDrops concoction Sharon had for a situation like *this*.

Pattycakes

Detective John Shannon of the Miami PD was tying the ribbon at the end of the second braid on his four-year-old daughter, Felicia, as she swirled the cinnamon and brown sugar into her oatmeal at breakfast.

"Don't play with your oatmeal—eat it," John admonished.

"I don't like it. It's squishy."

"Daddy Lorenzo made it especially good today. To warm you to your toes."

Felicia laughed, "My toes don't need warming. I got shoes."

"Well, eat it anyway." John turned to his partner. "I don't know, maybe you can get her to eat it. I gotta go."

"I da' know. Like she would pay any more attention to me than to you."

Lorenzo was the stay-at-home dad these days as his law firm had recently downsized, leaving Lorenzo scrambling through the want ads and making endless calls to his business associates looking for work.

John gave a playful tug to both of Felicia's braids and gave her a kiss on the top of her head. "Bye, sweetie. Be good and mind Daddy Lorenzo."

"K," Felicia answered as she reached for her coloring book across the table.

"Not till after you eat *all* your breakfast," Lorenzo scolded, grabbing the book from her hand.

"You're gonna have a handful today, I can tell," John whispered to Lorenzo as he gave him a quick kiss on his ear.

"Yeah, thanks. Be careful out there. Don't let the bad guys score any points today," Lorenzo called after the departing John, just as Felicia knocked over what was left of her milk.

☆☆☆

Detective Shannon was working on a case of massive identity theft with his partner, Connie Mata. They were a good team. They had been paired together because they were both gay, but they had transcended the labels and tackled their cases with street smarts and a sense of humor that led to a higher than average arrest rate.

They had been working this case on and off for over a month now, but with little success. Connie was working on the check-cashing angle. She had been tracking where bogus checks were being cashed using stolen identities taken from the heisted database of a Minneapolis accounting firm. She had been able to identify a cluster of bad checks cashed near Bal Harbour, an exclusive Miami community that seemed an unlikely location for such activity. She had only two leads. A security camera had captured an image of a suspect departing a deli just after one of the bad checks had been cashed. The suspect was wearing a large hat that covered the person's face, and it could not be determined if it was a man or a woman. The second piece of evidence was a photo from a home decorating shop of an old Oldsmobile that had pulled away just as the clerk realized they had been scammed and took a picture of the departing car. Unfortunately, there was no license plate visible, and though it was an old car, it was also a common model and thus difficult to trace. And John had also come to a dead end with his efforts to untangle the computer links used in stealing the database.

It looked like they would have to rely on one of their most basic police investigation techniques—questioning door to door—hoping they could get some hit of recognition from their two photos. They had mapped out sections of Bal Harbour and were taking one at a time. They had covered two so far without any luck. Today they were going to spend the morning canvassing a third area. It was near the beach in a nice older section. It was a pleasant morning, and they figured they could have pulled much tougher duty. So they stopped for some coffee and drove their unit on over to the first street they wanted to check out.

It was a short block that ended in a cul-de-sac. These were large Miami-style Spanish properties with ample yards, established tropical trees, and long drives leading up to the entrances. They walked up the drive of the first house on the left and rang the doorbell. It was answered by a frantic-looking housekeeper. The officers showed her their badges and asked if they might ask some questions.

"No English. No lady home. Go. No English."

"*Hablo español...*" Connie offered. But the lady had already slammed the door shut.

"Well, that was fun," Connie laughed.

"Okay, number two."

They trudged on over to the next house. They rang the bell. The door was answered almost immediately by an electric-blonde lady in her fifties. Even though it was almost ten thirty, she was still in her bathrobe.

"Oh...you're not the water heater man, are you?"

"No ma'am. Miami PD. We're doing some investigations in the neighborhood and wondered if we might ask you a few questions?" John asked.

The lady hesitated for a moment, considering. "Oh sure, come on in. Why the hell not. Got nothin' else to do."

She led the way into a glitzy, golden living room, offering the officers chairs opposite the sofa where she had been served a breakfast tray on the coffee table. She collapsed into the sofa as if it was a vast snow bank. "It's brekkie time." She stared at the tray before her, and then remembering her manners, asked, "You want breakfast?" She looked up at Connie and John.

"No thanks. We had that quite some time ago," Connie answered.

"Well, then..." The lady looked once again at her breakfast tray, picked up a glass of orange juice, and took a sip. She reacted sharply, calling out, "Temple! Temple!'

A diminutive Filipina ran into the room. "Yes? Yes? You want?"

"Temple, honey, what is this?" the lady asked, holding out the glass of orange juice like it was radioactive.

"OJ, lady."

"No, no, it's a screwdriver without the vodka." She waggled her hand. "Come on now, make this right." She handed the glass to Temple who scurried off. The lady leaned back into the folds of the sofa and tried focusing on the officers.

"Now then, what can I do for you two gentlemen?"

Connie ignored the remark and held out the photos. "We would like you to take a look at these photos. There have been some forged checks in the neighborhood recently due to identity theft. These photos were taken of what we believe may be the suspect. We were wondering if you might recognize either the person or the car."

"Oh honey. I *never* go out. I have a condition, you see."

"I know these are not the best pictures, but have you ever seen this car in the area? Maybe you look out the windows occasionally?" Connie added, with just a hint of snark.

"I'm sorry."

Just then, Temple came tipping back with the screwdriver.

"Oh thank you, dear." She took a sip and leaned back, closing her eyes. "I think we're done here," the lady sighed heavily.

John rose and motioned to Connie.

The lady looked up again at the officers. "Honey, would you show these gentlemen out, please. I don't think I can get up just now."

"You come." Temple waved to Connie and John.

"Thank you for your time, ma'am." John nodded. They followed.

There were only these two houses before the road ended at the cul-de-sac where cars could turn around. John looked at the grove of trees, vines, and tropical plants bordering the end of the road. He was surprised there was no house there. He was just about to cross the street to the next house on the other side when he stopped and peered into the growth. He could just make out a two-story house set way back from the street, mostly hidden by the jungle.

"Hey, let's take a look in there." John nudged Connie as they were crossing the street. They penetrated the darkness as they passed along an almost hidden walkway. They came to a dilapidated Spanish-style bungalow with a red tile roof, overgrown with bougainvillea and obscured by towering banana trees.

"Wow, this is a relic of the old Miami. Not many of these left anymore," John commented, as he brushed aside a hibiscus branch ablaze with scarlet flowers. He knocked on the door, as there was no bell.

The first thing they heard was the insane screeching of parrots and cockatoos in response to the knock. Then a woman's voice called out from inside, "Who is it?"

"Miami PD. We have just a few questions about an investigation we're conducting. Won't take but a minute or two of your time," Connie answered.

"Okay, gimme a moment. I'm not dressed yet. Just wait. Just wait."

"That's fine. We'll wait," John responded.

Finally, the door opened. Standing there was a woman who had to be at least forty, but she was wearing a long blue gingham baby doll dress with a bib and straps over a white frilly blouse with puff sleeves. On her feet, she had little white socks, folded over with pink trim, and red pumps covered in burgundy sequins with a little bow where the shoe met the sock. Her long hair, which was obviously a wig, fell forward over her shoulders in long braids.

"Hi, I'm Pattycakes Fontenet. It's pronounced Fontenet with an *A* at the end, not Fontenet with a *T*. Won't you come in?"

Pattycakes led the two officers into the large living room. It was painted a bright pink. Tropical birds flew free throughout. Parrots screeched and called out various obscene phrases. Pattycakes indicated the officers should sit on the sofa. A cockatoo waddled along the back of the sofa with a plastic ring in its beak, nodding as it jumped onto John's shoulder.

"Don't mind him," Pattycakes exclaimed. "He's just being friendly."

"The reason we're here..." Connie started to say.

"I bet you're wondering about my name—Pattycakes. Well, my real name is Patty, of course, but my daddy used to call me Pattycakes and it just stuck." She sighed. "He was such a good daddy."

"We'd just like to ask a few questions now if you don't mind. Don't want to waste any of your precious time," John continued.

"Now my mama was a darlin' too. I take after her, of course. She was a Georgia Beaufort—from Savannah. Such a charmin' personality. Had the daintiest feet. Like little paws."

"Ma'am..." John tried to get in.

"Isn't this a precious house?"

"Very nice. Now if you'll just let me get to the point..."

"My daddy built this. Used to own all the property right down to the beach. But had to parcel it off over the years. So sad. There's a canal that comes right up to the back of the house here. He had a discreet little dock right there. Daddy had interests in Cuba before the revolution. Used to import cigars till—well, you know." She whispered. "The embargo. Drove poor Daddy to distraction. Then he turned to rum...importing, not drinking. Used the little dock out back to bring in the rum late at night. Stored it in the cellar. But it was never the same. Did him in."

Connie leaned forward and held out the photos to Pattycakes. "If you'll just take a look at these, we need to know if you recognize anything about the subjects."

Pattycakes threw her hands up in the air. "Oh, pictures. I love pictures. Wait, wait." She shot up from her chair and raced over to a bookcase where a scarlet macaw was climbing up the side, latching his beak on each shelf to hoist himself up. "You're just gonna love these." She scurried back to her chair, plunking down a photo album in her lap and flipping through the pages.

"Miss Fontenet, if I could just..." John struggled to butt in.

"That's Fontenet with an *A*, not Fontenet with a *T*." She reminded him, even though he had pronounced it correctly.

"I understand that," he answered testily, "but we need to get your response to these photos—please."

"Look at that. Look at that." She foisted the album forward toward the detectives, open to a page full of snapshots. "See. That's me."

Two parrots got into a fight over some banana on the mantelpiece at the fireplace. They flapped their wings in a violent fit and tangled in wild cries—one finally flying away, eventually clinging to a tapestry.

"Wasn't I just the cutest little princess? My, my. What a gorgeous creature."

Connie and John looked at each other and shook their heads. They were obviously not going to get anywhere with this. Might just was well cross this one off their list.

"Thank you for your time, ma'am," John finally said, rising and leading the way toward the front door, depositing the cockatoo on a lampshade covered in bird poop.

"Oh, but you haven't seen me in my ballerina tutu. Such long legs. Balanchine said I coulda been a star."

"I'm sure you were a regular doll," Connie tossed out as they exited and closed the door gratefully behind them.

☆☆☆

Pattycakes tiptoed to the front door, peeking out the peephole to make sure the officers were on their way to the street. She smiled and pulled off her wig.

"It works every time." She chuckled and unzipped the baby doll dress, which she could very quickly put on or shed in one piece. She sped to one of the upstairs rooms, opened the door, and glanced in at a bank of computer screens, which were flashing the results of her multiple searches looking for financial database systems to hack.

☆☆☆

John got about three quarters of the way down the walk to the street. He stopped and rubbed his nose—a sign that he was thinking.

"What?" Connie came up to him, knowing this gesture.

John turned and looked back at the house. He walked a little way through the jungle to the side of the property where there was an old driveway. He looked back and saw a car parked with a tarp over it.

"What you thinking?" Connie grabbed his arm.

"Stay here. Keep an eye out. I'll be right back."

Connie gave a gesture. "So? So?"

John left Connie behind as he went to the cruiser and was some time on the radio to dispatch. When he climbed out of the car, he looked around the street and saw a FedEx truck making a delivery. Connie could see him chatting with the driver and finally the two came over to the house.

"Come with me," he indicated to Connie.

"Will you please tell me what's going on?"

31

"I got a hunch. Let's go over here and watch." John led her to the side of the house where they could see the front door, but could not be seen from inside.

The FedEx driver knocked on the door.

"Who is it?" a familiar voice called from inside.

"FedEx."

Pattycakes opened the door again, but this time she was barefoot, with short hair, and dressed in a T-shirt and shorts.

"Yeah? What ya got for me?" she asked.

"I'm here for the pickup."

"What? No, no. No pickup here. Wrong house." She took a quick scan out the door to see if there was anyone else about, but she did not see the carefully hidden detectives. She quickly retreated behind her door and locked it.

John waved a "thank you" to the driver as he went on back to his truck.

A big smile came over John.

"Okay, so she's changed clothes. Will you now please tell me what's going on?" Connie pushed.

"I called in for a search warrant. Should be here soon. Stay here and keep an eye out, and I'll go to the car and wait for it. Soon as we get it we're going in." He ginned at her, knowing she was desperate to know the plan, but he was not giving anything away—yet.

Very shortly, a police cruiser arrived and pulled up behind John's car. John went over and took the warrant from the officer.

"May need some backup. Stick around," John indicated.

"Sure thing." The officer got out of the car.

They walked to the side of the property, out of the line of sight from the front door. Connie joined them.

"Okay, here's the play. Connie, you go out back. Sergeant, you go to the side door by the drive. I'm going to serve the warrant, and if she tries to bolt, take her down."

"Still wish you'd tell me what's going on here," Connie griped.

"Yeah, yeah, yeah. Haven't got time now. You'll know in a minute. Go."

The two took up their positions. John went to the front door and knocked.

"What?" Pattycakes called from behind the door. She sounded pissed at being bothered once again.

"It's Detective Shannon, Miss Fontenet. I have a search warrant. I need to search your house."

John could hear a mumbled, "Oh shit," from behind the door, followed by a scurrying and the loud, raucous shrieks of the birds as Pattycakes scrambled to escape.

"She's coming out," John called out to Connie and the sergeant. He dashed to the side of the house and just caught sight of Pattycakes fleeing from the back door and racing down toward the dock in the canal where she had a speedboat set for a quick getaway.

Connie dashed after her—tackling and throwing Pattycakes face down with a thump. Connie had the cuffs on her in no time. John went over to the covered car, removed the tarp, and there it was—the Oldsmobile in the photo.

Connie and the sergeant searched the house and found the room of roving computers, bogus checks, and a stack of credit card applications waiting to be filled out with stolen names. Pattycakes sat glumly on the sofa in her living room.

"Who's gonna take care of my babies?" she asked John, indicating her birds.

"I've called animal services. They'll be okay."

Pattycakes studied John a moment and then asked, "So what tipped you off, huh?"

"Dorothy's ruby slippers." John smiled. "Something just nagged at me after we left the first time. Then I remembered that back in 2005 a pair of the *Wizard of Oz* shoes had been swiped from the Judy Garland Museum in Grand Rapids. And I figured you might have been the one involved, or at least bought them on the black market. They were insured for a million bucks, you know. Don't know why you would wear them around the house, though, being that valuable."

"Well, a little vanity, I guess." She looked at John for a moment. "Damn, you're a gay cop. Am I right?"

"Yes, ma'am, gay as a giggle."

Pattycakes shook her head. "Just my luck. A gay cop is the only one who could catch me out. But hey, it was a good ride while it lasted."

"Nice little act by the way, Miss Pattycakes—liked the Dorothy drag. Had me fooled me for a while."

"Well, you know what they say. Gotta have fun with your work."

"You should be a writer. Great imagination. But you'll have plenty of time for that later—in prison."

☆☆☆

It was after six o'clock by the time John got back home. Felicia came rushing at him. "Did you bring me a present, Daddy John?" she asked, indicating the paper bag under his arm.

'No, honey. This is something from Daddy's work. Did I miss dinner?" he asked Lorenzo.

"Nope." Lorenzo indicated the set dinner table. He came over and gave John a hug. "Just about to serve. Wash up."

John set the paper bag down on the dining table and went to the bathroom. When he returned, Lorenzo was serving up dinner, and Felicia came shuffling up to him and grabbed his leg.

"Oh, Daddy John, these are just *so* great." She was prancing around in the ruby slippers.

"Oh no, honey. Those are not for you. They're evidence from work. I have to do some computer research on these this evening. Please take them off now."

Felicia burst into tears. She scurried to her room and slammed the door.

Lorenzo turned to John and laughed. "Well, sweetie, solving a major crime will seem like a piece of cake next to persuading Felicia to give *those* back."

Silverskin

Luke Tender strode up the walkway to the modest house with the imposing front porch. Arching elm trees created a cavern of shade along the street on this sweltering July afternoon. Handsome Luke was dressed in his finest Armani lightweight summer suit, crisp white shirt, and Valentino tie. He knocked soundly on the screen door and waited for a response. The knock was quickly answered by a slight woman in her early fifties. Her hair was covered by a floral scarf, tied at the back, as they tend to do in Indiana when cleaning house.

"Oh, Mr. Tender," she greeted, smiling, "do come in; he's expecting you." She pushed open the screen door wide, giving an awkward curtsy, and admitted Luke. The door snapped smartly shut behind. Luke stood for a moment savoring the cool of the dark entryway with its slatted wainscot painted a pale yellow. Luke took in the surroundings. Not that much different from when he had been here as a kid of fourteen.

"Laura, how's your papa doing?" Luke asked in a discreet voice, in case Red was close by.

"Oh, you know...best as can be expected. The stroke sorta shook us all up a bit. Doctors say he's about as good as he's going to get." She pointed toward the living room, the blinds drawn against the heat and glare.

"How *you* doin'? Been keeping yourself fit?" Luke asked, putting a hand on Laura's shoulder.

She smiled with a noncommittal shrug, and disappeared down the hall toward the back of the house and the continuation of her chores. "I'll bring the iced tea in a little while," she said and gave a wave just before she disappeared.

Luke stood for a moment in the silence. The house smelled just as he remembered it—cabbage, carpet mildew, and furniture polish. He

35

hesitated a moment before entering the living room, took a breath, and then plunged forward.

Red was hunched over in a wheelchair, barely regarding the flickering television where he was positioned. Luke walked over, turned off the set, and pulled up a chair to face Red.

"Well, well, well, you sure are one tough old dog, aren't you?" Luke opened.

Red looked up with a twisted smile. He had lost a lot of weight because of the stroke and looked like an old discarded suit. He was a big man, with beefy hands, and towered over the eighteen-year-old Luke all those many years ago. He was almost completely bald, except for a Brillo fringe of red hair. He was most exactly *not* what you would expect a hairdresser to look like in a small Indiana town.

Red reached over and patted Luke's hand. He tried to speak but all that came out was an awkward tumble of sounds.

Luke nodded. "That's okay, Red, no need to talk. But you can listen. Let me tell you all the news."

☆☆☆

Waynesboro, Indiana was a small agricultural town buried in the hinterlands of rural Indiana. The locals pronounced it "Winesbura." Luke Tender was fourteen and worked after school in his father's butcher shop, cutely named Tender Cuts. But Luke figured half the town's population didn't even get the play on words on his family name. Luke was a smart kid. But he had recently had a growth spurt, and his parts were all mismatched. He had big ears that stood out from the side of his head like the plywood clown with the big mouth that one putted through at the miniature golf park out by the Dairy Queen. His nose was too long, and his hair grew in six different directions, like a wheat field plummeted by a hailstorm. And he had terrible zits. His arms were too long, and he had already outgrown the jeans bought just six months ago. His poor dad shook his head at his patchwork kid and despaired of any girl ever finding him attractive. He sorely remembered how mean kids could be to one other. But he also forgot how quickly kids could grow into themselves and change out of an awkward stage.

36

Luke's mother had died giving birth to his sister when he was four, and he could hardly remember her now. His father managed the butcher shop, took care of the two kids, and still found time to volunteer at the Little League, attend the Rotary, and play poker on Wednesday nights with the guys from International Harvester.

Dad was tying up a Sunday roast for Mrs. Meeks, as Luke struggled with a side of lamb on the butcher block in the back of the shop. He had been instructed to cut it up, as Easter was fast approaching, and many of the customers wanted lamb for their holiday table.

"How's it going?" his father asked, as he came through the plastic strips separating the front of the shop from the back. He leaned over to look at what Luke was doing. He nodded approval. "Looks good, but see that?" He pointed to the translucent membrane covering the leg of lamb.

"Yes, sir," Luke responded.

"Silverskin—nasty stuff. Gotta get that trimmed off. Gotta let the meat be free. Gotta let it breathe. Here." Dad took the slender knife from Luke, slipped it under the membrane, and expertly sliced it away. "There, think you can do that?"

"Sure, Dad," Luke smiled.

"Doin' a great job there, lad."

Luke felt as if he, himself, was covered in silverskin. But he didn't know how to perform the dexterous self-surgery required to remove it. Luke was pretty sure he was gay. But he had no idea what to do with this awkward bit of knowledge. He didn't feel damaged. He didn't feel guilty. Confused, yes. Horny, yes. But he had no idea where to find others like him. This was Indiana, for chriz sake, before the lure of the Internet. And there were certainly no gay bars, Gay-Straight Alliances, or pride parades in his neck of the woods. What little he did know about gay life resided in the common stereotypes of the time—florists, hairdressers, airline stewards. That was about the extent of his knowledge about gay life.

He needed a strategy. He knew he couldn't rely on any of his friends for advice. They would drop him like a hot stone if he came out to any of them, or asked any of them for advice. What about teachers? He had a crush on his English teacher, Mr. Rightmeyer, and suspected he might be one of the tribe, but didn't have the courage to come out to him, either. Now the town florist was a lady, and there were no airline stewards this side of Indianapolis, so that left only one other possibility—Caulder Stark, the hairdresser at Quick Cuts Fashion Emporium, on Main Street, next to the pharmacy. Yeah, that's what he'd do. Next time he needed a haircut he would shun Mr. Trimble, his father's sixty-year-old barber, and head straight on over to Quick Cuts.

Luke was so nervous about this he kept putting off getting his hair cut till his father finally called him out on it and insisted he get his hair cut, or he would take the shears to Luke himself.

Luke promised his dad he would go for a cut on Wednesday, but missed that day *and* Thursday. Finally, under the threat of corporal punishment he relented and headed on over to Quick Cuts Friday afternoon after school.

With his heart in his mouth, he quietly entered the shop. Lucinda May, who did nails two days a week, was intently engrossed with Mrs. Warner's extensions as Luke slipped into Mr. Stark's chair.

"What'll it be, young man?" Mr. Stark asked, slipping the smock he used for his clients over Luke's slender shoulders. "Let me guess, you need a haircut, am I right?" he asked, as he took the comb to Luke's tangled mass of shaggy dark hair. "Boy, you got cowlicks growin' every which way but Sunday."

"That's what I've been told."

"I got some great stuff you could use on that acne of yours," he added, as he took the clippers to the back of Luke's neck. "How come I never seen you in here before? Huh?"

Luke didn't answer, and was silent during the rest of the haircut, as he wrestled with what he was going to say to Mr. Stark after the cut was over. He didn't want to spill his confession out in front of Lucinda May and Mrs. Warner. He had to figure out how to get Mr. Stark into the back of the shop where he could talk privately. Luke kept glancing in the mirror at Mr. Stark. He had never really seen a gay man up close before, and he minutely examined him for any obvious "signs" of his being gay.

Did he purse his lips? Did he flourish with his hands? Did he wear eye makeup? But Luke was having a really hard time finding anything that he could latch on to. Seemed like just some regular Joe to him.

As Mr. Stark was brushing him down with the big, soft talc brush after the cut, Luke asked, "You were telling me you got some acne stuff..."

"Oh yeah..." He disappeared into the back of the shop. Luke followed after.

"Oh, you can wait out front. I'll be right there."

"Please, sir, can I have a word with you?" Luke asked, very nervous now, but his heart pounded with some urgency.

Mr. Stark must have been able to see that Luke was concerned about something. "Sure, what's up?"

There was an old sofa on one side of the back room and a coat rack with smocks dangling like deflated ghosts. Mr. Stark indicated Luke should sit. "Okay, son, what can I do you for?" Luke was suddenly afraid Mr. Stark might make a pass at him and didn't know what he'd do if that happened.

"Well, I...ah. I...ah..."

"Come on—out with it. I'm not going to bite." Mr. Stark pulled up a chair in front of Luke and sat down, giving him his full attention.

"Well, sir...I'm...I'm that way. You know."

"No, what way is that?" Mr. Stark was truly puzzled.

"I don't know who else to talk to about it."

Mr. Stark was becoming impatient. "Son, you've got to speak up and tell me what's troubling you. I can't read your mind."

Luke stopped and looked intently at Mr. Stark. "Well sir, I'm like you."

Now Mr. Stark was even more puzzled. "How's that? A Democrat—overweight—an Episcopalian?"

Luke sighed with frustration. "No, sir, I may be gay, and I need to talk to someone else who is gay too."

Mr. Stark slapped his knees and roared with laughter. Luke was mortified and stood up to leave. Mr. Stark waved him back down. "Son, son, sit down. I'm not laughing at you. Really." He put his hand on

Luke's shoulder. "Kid, I'm not gay."

"You're not? But you're a hairdresser."

That set Mr. Stark off laughing even harder. He nodded, "Yes, yes, yes, yes. I know. But, son, that doesn't mean I'm automatically gay. The world doesn't work that way." He thought a moment. "Oh my, it just never ceases to amaze me how silly and closed-minded people can be sometimes." Luke looked shocked. "Oh no, not you, son. You're too young to know any better. It's the people around you—this town, this state, this world." He looked down and thought for a moment. "But that doesn't concern you, does it? What you want to know is how do *you* deal with being yourself. Isn't that it?"

"Yeah. That's about right."

"So how can I help you?"

"Do you know of anybody else like me?" Luke asked with such a plaintive plea. "I really need to talk to someone."

"Well there are the two ladies over on C Street."

"Yeah, but they're *ladies*," Luke complained.

"See what you mean. Not much help for you there, I'd guess."

"Mr. Stark..." Luke began.

"Hey, call me Red. That's what everybody calls me."

Luke didn't continue, but looked crestfallen and helpless. Red thought for a moment and then spoke up. "Now don't get your shorts in an uproar. Thinkin' there might be sumpin' I might be able to do for ya."

Luke looked up with a hopeful smile. "Yeah?"

"First of all, take this." He handed Luke a tube of acne cream from a storeroom shelf. "You're never gonna get a boyfriend lookin' like that."

"I only got a dollar for the haircut," Luke explained.

"Not to worry. It's all on the house today—new customer discount."

Luke gave a big grin as he stood up to go. "Gee, thanks, Mr. Red."

"Now you get along. And don't feel sorry for yourself, okay."

"I won't."

"Give me your telephone number. I got an idea that might help. Will give you a call when I get sumpin' lined up. You free Saturday evenings?"

"Yes, sir."

☆☆☆

There was Mr. Gardner, from the hardware. And Clement Hardy, the pharmacist. And from the train depot, Warner Stevens, who sold tickets. And there was even a junior from his high school, Paul Loomis. And finally, the small group was finished off by a salesman from John Deere, Burton Marcy.

"Come on in," Red urged Luke, as he hesitated at the door to Red's living room. Luke edged into the room, guided by Red. "You said you wanted to meet some folks like yourself, so I did a little scouting around and invited these fine fellas."

Luke was amazed—he knew them all. Some were friends of his father; all were well-regarded citizens—and all were gay? Luke couldn't believe it.

"Come on in, baby; don't be shy." Burton patted the empty chair next to him, flashing a big smile.

"Ooooh, somebody likes Kentucky Fried Chicken," Clement Hardy acidly commented, as Luke inched his way toward the group, not at all sure how to react to all of this.

"Now gentlemen, behave yourselves." Red took hold of Luke's arm and led him to a chair next to Paul. "We have a young man here who simply needs some help in figuring out how this gay business works. So save your cattiness for your potlucks, and let's give this young fella a helping hand. Okay?"

Luke leaned in toward Red and whispered, "Thank you."

That night Luke found his standing. The event went far better than he could ever have hoped for. After the initial nervousness from the whole group, they were able to settle into some really fun and constructive conversations. Luke got some good advice from the men and made some new friends—and especially one.

Paul befriended Luke and helped him deal with the rigors of being gay in high school. Their friendship blossomed and continued through college and the beginning of Luke's medical studies in Bloomington, where Paul was teaching economics at Indiana University. They became a couple and founded an organization to help young gay and questioning

41

teens.

Red had shepherded Luke through the rest of his high school year and had helped set up a scholarship fund for Luke to go to college. Luke did indeed grow into himself and was the handsome and engaging young man now sitting with Red this summer afternoon.

Though Red could not speak coherently, he could still write, and had a small chalkboard he used to scratch out terse messages.

Good boy, Red scribbled in response to Luke's recital of his current life.

"Thank you," Luke responded verbally.

How's Paul? Red wrote.

"He's just great. We both are."

Medical studies?

Luke nodded. "Very good. Just another year before I start interning."

Red seemed to hesitate. He looked for a long time at Luke and rubbed at the chalkboard with his hand to erase the last message. But he didn't start writing right away. Luke gave him an encouraging look, trying to lead him into further conversation, however limited.

"You okay?" Luke leaned in.

Red gave an almost imperceptible shake of his head and looked down. He scribbled. *Help me.*

"Of course, anything." Luke leaned closer.

End this, Red scratched.

Luke sat back, confounded with the request. Did he misunderstand? "You mean...? You want...?"

Red nodded.

Luke shook his head. "I can't do that, Red; you know that."

Red wrote angrily, *I helped u.*

"Yes, I know. But that was to help me expand my life. You want me now to end a life. It's not the same, Red. I can't do that."

Red looked at him with great pain in his eyes but nodded that he understood.

Just then, Laura came in with a tray of iced tea. She put it on the piano behind Luke. She handed a glass to Luke and then went to her father.

"Daddy, I fixed the tea the way you asked me to." Her voice quivered and her hand was shaking as she handed him the tea. Red looked up at her with a faint smile. She leaned over and kissed him on the forehead.

Luke looked at her as she left the room, and then, realizing what she had just done, spun around to Red. But it was too late. Red was draining the last of the glass of tea. He leaned back against the chair and closed his eyes.

Luke's first reaction was to spring up and try to get Red to the hospital so he could have his stomach pumped. But he paused and sat back down.

Red opened his eyes and wrote, *thank u*. He closed his eyes once again, and his head fell forward and his breathing rapidly slowed.

Luke was sad. Luke was happy.

Welcome to Good-bye

Clair thinks Abigail is an aggressive, greedy bitch. That's because Abigail covets Brandon's very valuable Picasso dove drawing. Abigail insists Brandon said it was meant for her before he died, but Clair refuses to acknowledge the bequest. Brandon told Abigail he acquired it from the Master himself after a night of communal drinking in a string of French bars in the late sixties, and Brandon said it perfectly captured her youthful spirit and meant for her to have it when he died. He had, in fact, signed the frame's backing to that effect. However, Clair had scratched out that little detail and continues to play dumb. And as Clair was once married to Brandon, she asserts hereditary possession and refuses to acknowledge Abigail's legitimate claim. It is all very clumsy and messy. However, the will was to be read later that afternoon, and who knew what surprises the crafty Brandon might have devised. But Clair was certain it would all be sorted out in her favor.

"More Champagne, dear?" Claire was poised with the bottle of chilled wine over Abigail's nearly empty glass.

"So gracious." Abigail smiled, accepting the offer and then abruptly turning away to chat with Melissa Stapleton, the cartoonist who penned the very successful comic strip *Scrappy*, featuring the adventures of a feisty, hard-assed pooch—syndicated in 180 newspapers nationwide. She had made a fortune on Scrappy books, plush stuffed Scrappys, Scrappy coffee mugs, and Scrappy calendars.

"How in the world *do* you ever come up with all those clever, original ideas? Just imagine a new strip every single day. It must be exhausting," Abigail commented, looking over Melissa's shoulder as the hunky Grover Farley sauntered over from the kitchen area. Abigail knew him by sight from many SoHo gallery openings, but they had never been properly introduced. She was determined, however, to rectify that grave error immediately.

Melissa started to answer, but Abigail was already on her way over to corral Grover up against Brandon's massive desk.

"Abigail Williams." She smiled, extending her hand to Grover. "I don't believe we've met before. How did you know Brandon?"

"We used to fuck." Grover beamed, so pleased with himself for his shocking honesty.

"Oh my." Abigail's eyes widened, and she backed away, blushing, but delighted to have some juicy new gossip. Now this was a whole new dimension to the Brandon so cherished and beloved by the women of the New York literary world. She could hardly wait to rush over to Bunny Feldman with the Breaking Eyewitness News. But she bumped right into, and was thwarted by, Milton Sauer, literary critic for *The Uptown Courier*.

"Abby, you sweet, darling, delicious thing, you. How *have* you been keeping yourself?" Milton did a little torch dance in front of her, all three hundred and twenty pounds of him—a jolly, prancing Ganesha. He was obviously sloshed.

"Milton, cool it." She rushed past him and headed again toward Bunny. But Bunny was now intimately engrossed in conversation with Tabby Raught, who Abigail *absolutely could not stand*. The news for Bunny would just have to wait for now.

"Wasn't it a lovely memorial service?" Carson whispered in Abigail's ear with his sardine breath, as he leaned forward and took her arm in his clammy hand. "At least it didn't rain. Tell me, why it is that in almost every movie where there is a funeral it is always raining? I mean, even if it was set in the middle of the Sahara Desert, they would depict it raining at a funeral. Why is that, do you think? Huh? Did you ever think about that? All those black umbrellas bunched up together like barnacles on the bottom of a boat." Carson adjusted his thick glasses and ran his hand over his oily, slicked hair. He reached over again and ran his moist hand up Abigail's arm toward her shoulder.

"I haven't the slightest idea, Carson," she answered, pulling away from his grip and heading toward the buffet table. The revelation of this *secret side* of Brandon had fragmented and scattered her. She wondered how long Brandon had been this way. Had he dallied with men when *they* were still together? Had he been cruising the streets of the West Village on his way back from the deli whenever he said he was going out to pick up a pack of smokes or a ham and cheese sub? Was he picking up men instead?

She tried to compose herself with a spoonful of tender caviar on a water cracker with chopped egg, a sprinkle of finely diced onion, and a squeeze of lemon. How the finer delicacies of life soothed her turbulent landscape. She took a deep breath and another sip of Champagne. Ah, now that was much better.

Brandon Bonaventura—renowned author, a fixture of the New York literary and arts social scene, world traveler, cavalier lover, and cherished friend—lived a well ordered and somewhat fastidious life. His wife, Clair, and his other occasional romantic partners often complained about his obsessive-compulsive need to have his world ordered *exactly* to his liking, no matter how his partners felt, or what they wanted.

For example, he always slept with the bedroom windows wide open, even on the coldest January night (infuriating everyone), and piled a Cascade mountain range of blankets and comforters over himself, with just his eyes and nose peeking out of the little cave constructed around his head. He looked like a blind mole investigating new frontiers. As a consequence, Brandon always placed his slippers by the side of his bed in a very exact and precise arrangement, which no one dare disturb, so that when he got up in the morning he could slip his feet into the warm, fuzzy slippers without touching the cold concrete floor, even if he was still half asleep.

Having grown up in Minnesota, he had become accustomed to cold, bracing air and suffered greatly when he visited the tropics. He needed to crank up the AC to minus twenty below to fall asleep.

He had a very fixed routine on the days he wrote. Up at six. Gallons of coffee, with a breakfast of fruit, yogurt, and the *New York Times*. And, still in his pajamas, he padded across the loft to his desk by the big windows overlooking the Hudson River.

Never able to segue from longhand to computer, he still wrote out his novels, essays, and short stories on yellow legal pads. He had a secretary, trained by years of exposure to his felt tip hieroglyphics, to type out his manuscripts every afternoon when he napped or went shopping at the local farmer's market.

However, he *was* an avid fan of the Internet's search capabilities and often used his laptop for detailed investigations. Early in his career, he had spent endless hours in various NYC libraries doing his extensive research for whatever opus he was currently working on—and that was precious time away from his urgent writing projects. Nowadays it was just a quick log-on, and he could be surfing the world, naked, with Bach cranked up till the windows rattled.

This morning he was barefoot in shorts and a T-shirt. The windows were open to let in the soft summer morning breeze, and Bossa Nova was sexing in the background. He arched his back to relieve the pain. He thought he might have to get a new chair, or he might have reached up to grab something on a high shelf in the wrong way. He had been noticing a discomfort in his back for about a month now.

He turned to his legal pad. He stared at it as he focused and unfocused his eyes, trying to get a clearer read on what he had scribbled out yesterday, but he realized it wasn't so much his sight as it was his mind. He looked at what he had written, but he couldn't make any sense of it. It was as if it was written in Hebrew. Not a good start to a morning of writing. He struggled for half an hour and then decided it would be better to do some research instead. He jiggled his mouse to awaken his computer and began to research the symptoms of pancreatic cancer. The wife of Brancusi—his main character—was about to be dispatched, so his hero would be free to travel to Lebanon, where he would soon discover a lost stone tablet, which would enable the hero to decipher the mysterious language of Atlantis, eventually leading to a vast undiscovered treasure. Brandon had decided pancreatic cancer would do the trick in dispatching the inconvenient wife, and he set out to research the symptoms of the disease.

Let's see now—loss of appetite, weight loss, yellowing of skin and whites of eyes, upper abdominal pain that radiates to the back, depression, blood clots. Okay, he could work with that. He printed out the research and laid it out in front of him on his desk to study. He leaned back in his chair and began to focus on his findings in earnest. *Huh*. Loss of appetite, yes, he had not been very hungry lately. Weight loss—he'd dropped twenty pounds in the last few months without dieting. And his eyes had looked very strange lately—bloodshot with a distinct daffodil tinge. And then there was the pain...He reached for the phone and made an appointment with his doctor.

Clair still had her key, and she let herself into Brandon's loft after he had not responded to her incessant knocking. She looked around as she entered. Even though it was late on a winter's afternoon there were no warm, welcoming lights. It was dreary and dark, every object in the loft edged with a silver-blue tinge. Had he been napping?

"Brandon!" she called out, maneuvering her way around the heavy furniture, stacks of magazines, books, and dirty clothes. What in the world had happened to him? He would never have allowed his living environment to become disordered like this when they were together. She ran her finger along the library table and collected a ploughed field of dust. She wiped it on a kitchen towel thrown over the back of a lounge chair. She paused, looked around the vastness of the loft, and sighed.

"In here, Clair," Brandon called out from his cubby of a bedroom, constructed at the far end of the loft, next to the kitchen.

Clair made her way into the even darker inner sanctum of Brandon's dream chamber, as he liked to call his bedroom. He was stretched out on his bed with a Guatemalan throw tucked up securely around his neck.

"Come sit by me," Brandon instructed, indicating a chair pulled up by the head of his bed in anticipation of her arrival. She made her way through the gloom and sat beside him very primly, hands folded on her lap. She felt like an orphaned character in a Dickens novel, awaiting final pronouncements (which would forever change her life) from a very rich, but dying great-aunt.

Brandon reached over toward the bedside table, fumbling for a piece of paper. He couldn't quite reach it. "Please…" He indicated the paper. Claire handed it to him, with a desperate urge to sneak a peek at it, but knew it would not go unnoticed if she did.

Brandon scooted himself into a seated position, turned on the bedside lamp, and struggled to put on his reading glasses. "Now, then…" He studied the paper a moment, but declined to speak further, as he seemed to be gathering his thoughts.

"Oh Brandon, what is all this silliness? Really, you've been totally unavailable to all your friends for months. Now you call me over here on this miserable afternoon for who knows *what*, and all you can do is slouch in bed and moan like a bored panda. Do you mind telling me what this is all about, please?"

He waved the piece of paper at her—a printout of his test results. "I have pancreatic cancer and have about two months to live. I thought it might be a good idea to get my affairs in order."

☆☆☆

Brandon had disappeared, unaccompanied, to Switzerland for a series of highly experimental monkey gland treatments that were the latest buzz in the alternative medical world for pancreatic cancer. He had never returned, and his attorney had announced that he had been cremated immediately after his death, in accordance with his wishes. His ashes had been shipped back to New York for the service at his loft this afternoon.

Clair had cheerfully assumed the role of Grieving Widow, even though she and Brandon had divorced ever so many years ago. But as she had been the only *official* spouse, she donned her widow's weeds with the air and grace of a sanctified Mary Magdalene. Clair attended to the catering, floating through the loft emptying ashtrays, pouring wine, and emitting occasional sighs, as she glanced up at the large David Hockney portrait of Brandon, draped in black crepe, hanging on the wall behind his desk. The service and the reading of the will, however, had been organized by Brandon's attorney, Eludio Martinez.

It was clear that Clair anticipated the bulk of Brandon's estate would come to her. She was already mentally redecorating the loft. That shabby kitchen definitely needed remodeling, and the bedroom needed opening out—too confined and dark. After all, wasn't it *her* that Brandon had called to his bedside to discuss "the arrangement of his affairs"? However, she held the contents of that discussion very close to her vest (because she really didn't know Brandon's final wishes). Not even Binky Thornton could pry any details out of Clair. And Binky had been Clair's Vassar roommate, and they *always* shared *everything*.

Meanwhile, on the other side of the loft, Abigail sported a smug smile of her own. She had shredded several cocktail napkins to confetti this afternoon in nervous anticipation of the reading of the will, but she remained confident that Brandon had held her *true and deep affection* close to his heart when he laid out his final plans. She had, in fact, already insured the Picasso dove drawing, feeling certain that she would be taking it home with her later that afternoon.

Now Grover had a secret smile of his own. As a struggling painter, of somewhat dubious talent, he had nonetheless flourished by charming any number of closeted, wealthy gentlemen with his gym-toned body, his Julia Roberts smile, and his Jeff Stryker endowment. And he rejoiced in the fact that Brandon, in particular, had a very special soft spot in his heart for this tousled, boyish rogue. He was certain he would walk away, at the very least, with the diamond Rolex watch. He knew exactly where it was stashed in the sock drawer and planned to slip by the dresser on his way back from the bathroom, if it wasn't bequeathed him in the will.

In fact, every guest had the heart of a Wall Street investment banker and had dreams of leaving the gathering with a very substantial bequest of their own. Every single item in the loft was spoken for many times over in the hearts and minds of the leering mourners.

A sudden a hush came over the entire assemblage as Eludio Martinez crossed to Brandon's desk with his briefcase. Now Eludio was a big man, not tall but fat. His shirt collar was too tight around his marshmallow neck, and his tie was not quite straight. He wiped his brow with a spotless white handkerchief his wife had so nicely ironed for him that morning. He looked up at the riveted, attentive crowd. No one stirred. Feeling the pressure, he fumbled with the clasp to the briefcase. Finally, he pulled out the document he was looking for. Slowly the crowd began to draw closer. Eludio took out his glasses case and smiled as he opened it and carefully slipped on his glasses.

"Now then..." He paused as he scanned the will in preparation for the reading. He looked up and asked, "Are we ready?" What a stupid question. "Okay, then. As Brandon's executor, I can report that the court has found the will to be in exact and correct order. It has been witnessed and signed by a notary. There is all the usual legal jargon at the beginning attesting to the sanity and sound mind of the author et cetera, et cetera." He looked up again.

"Okay, who gets what?" Clair boomed out over the deepening silence of the group.

"Yeah, yeah..." Eludio turned a few pages and came to the cogent part. He became a little nervous, anticipating the group's reaction. "Well, I want you all to understand that Brandon did not act under my advisement in this matter. He..."

"Just read the damn thing," Milton shouted out.

"Very well. It reads: *that I, Brandon Bonaventura, being of sound mind*—and all that you already know—*do hereby settle my estate in the following manner. All of you, who are gathered together here today for the reading of this will, are my very nearest and dearest. And it has been quite impossible for me to pick any one of you as my sole heir. Nor, in fact, is it possible for me to find any equitable way to divide up my estate amongst the many caring individuals that I know love me so dearly.*

So it is my intention to settle my estate in the following manner. First, after careful consideration, I rejected the idea of having Clair as executrix, to be responsible for distributing the many bequests to friends. I can just see her establishing separate little piles of goodies for each of you. She would then pause and consider each pile, and would, no doubt, rethink everything and start all over again, and nothing would ever get accomplished. Then I thought about making separate multiple bequests to each and every dear friend, but the list was too exhausting, and I just could not face the task in my deteriorating condition. So what I finally decided to do was to throw it all up in the air like a bursting piñata and to bequeath everything to everybody.

Every single person here in this room today (my attorney is exempt, of course) is heir to everything I own. Have fun deciding who gets what. And please, be ladies and gentlemen about this. I am sure none of you are greedy."

Eludio glanced up from the will. There was a moment of stark terror on the face of each guest. There was a beat of about two seconds, and then all hell broke loose.

"Don't you want to discuss this as a group first?" Eludio tried to speak above the stampede. "We can do this in an orderly fashion." But no one heard him.

Abigail shot forward in a mad dash toward the Picasso, with Clair in hot pursuit behind, both grabbing the framed drawing at the same time and engaging in a monumental tug of war. Milton waddled toward the Hockney, already perspiring profusely with even this limited effort. Grover slipped into the bedroom and quickly found the desired Rolex, slipping it into his coat pocket. Melissa began rummaging through Brandon's file drawers looking for the deed to the loft—she was no dummy, she was not about to waste her time on ashtrays and opera posters. Other guests were gathering silver, crystal, linens, small statues, and miscellaneous art works—anything they could fit into their purses or bags. There were not, as yet, any takers for the heavy furniture, as that would require a different set of logistics. But there were a few folks sticking masking tape with their names written on it on antique furniture pieces, staking out their claims.

Quietly, and without any notice, an elderly gentleman slipped into the loft. He walked to the center of the room and looked at the chaos and frenzy around him. People whipped by, annoyed that he was in their way and shoved him aside as they proceeded to strip the loft bare, but otherwise paying him no attention. Finally, he took a silver whistle out of his pocket and blew a sharp blast. The commotion froze. Everyone looked over to the man.

At first, there was no recognition, but then Clair was suddenly shaken into awareness. "Brandon?" she asked as she moved slowly toward him.

Now to be fair, Brandon was radically changed. He had lost a great deal of weight from his treatment and was as trim as a runner. He had forsaken his contact lenses for a very fashionable pair of French glasses, and his hair, which had been longish and dyed before, was now in a short Caesar cut—a handsome, natural silver.

"Greetings." Brandon laughed and surveyed the room. "Surprised to see me? Delighted? Horrified?" No one could respond. "No, I am not a ghost. Surprisingly, my treatment was very successful, as you can see, and I am now in full remission."

Clair came forward with a touch of anger. "What is this all about, Brandon? Why this charade of a funeral and a reading of the will? Why are you subjecting us to this?"

Brandon nodded and smiled, "What? No welcome home? No congratulations on your recovery? No how glad we are to see you all safe and sound?"

There was a tepid effort to respond, but it seemed a bit contrived, as everyone felt so embarrassed.

Brandon continued, "How many of you kept in touch with me during my treatment?" No one responded, but rather most looked away. "Who of you really cared about how I was doing?" A chorus of voices rang out with a parody of sincere concern. "Really?" he responded.

Brandon began a slow walk through his guests. Looking at each one, continuing with his narration. "So because of your apparent neglect, I decided to try a little experiment. I wanted to know just what love and friendship meant in this Great Recession age where the phrase 'friend me' has taken on a whole new meaning in cyberspace. Where anonymous friends are numbered in the hundreds, and where a real handshake or a kiss are never exchanged.

"You see, I wanted to know exactly how healthy my supposed friendships were. So my plan was to return from the dead and surprise you all with this little visit. I wanted to see what people really felt about me—not to my face, but behind my back. I wanted to see what was most important to you in our relationship. And you are all holding the proof of that right now in your hands. Thank you all for making it so abundantly clear to me."

"That's not fair, Brandon." Melissa stepped forward, now angry.

"We all thought you were dead. Here is the urn with your ashes—Mr. Martinez read the will—we all thought we were acting in good faith. I don't see how you can accuse us of being greedy, when you were the one who perpetrated this deception." The rest of the group responded in loud agreement.

Brandon considered her argument and nodded. "Yes, perhaps that is a fair assessment. I was deceptive. But, you see, it's not simply about how you treated me, but also how you treated each other.

"Now, I have a storage room right across the hall, and before you all arrived I had a video surveillance system installed so I could monitor this entire event. And it is quite clear to me now, from observing all of you, that you really are not very nice people." Everyone was looking around the room for the hidden cameras. "Yes, the cameras are everywhere, and with microphones as well. I suggest you might want to reflect in a private moment about how you all behaved today.

"And because I am *not* dead, the will is, of course, not in effect. And from what I have witnessed here today, I shall also make the will null and void.

"I find from my time of isolation in Switzerland that I have become quite content and comfortable being and living alone. And so, after you kindly return all of my possessions to their rightful places, I shall bid each and every one of you a very fond, but also a very permanent, good-bye.

☆☆☆

Finally, Brandon stood quietly alone in the middle of his loft—all the guests departed. The caterers were dismantling the buffet and cleaning up. He looked around at his still disordered home but sighed with great relief. He looked forward to getting back to his creative life once again. What a journey! He was now ready to embark on his new, much simpler life. But then he realized—with all his feisty old acquaintances gone, what in the world was he going to write about?

The Tribe Comes Together for a Sort of Moroccan Easter Feast

Delgado was tending to the two large legs of lamb. The butcher had butterflied them beautifully. Now they must marinate overnight. They would go onto the grill on the deck just as the guests were arriving for an Easter celebration around noon tomorrow. Delgado, who was from Argentina, had a way with grilled meats. And although this was going to be a Moroccan feast, Delgado was preparing the lamb in his own very special way. First, he had slathered the lamb with salt and pepper. Then he made a marinade of olive oil, tons of minced garlic, freshly grated ginger, soy sauce, and handfuls of freshly chopped rosemary. He laid out the lamb in two large, flat baking pans and poured the marinade over the lamb, turning it several times with tongs to make sure the lamb was entirely covered. He then placed plastic wrap over the pans and placed them in the refrigerator to infuse with flavor overnight.

Bryce and Delgado, who were both in their mid-thirties, lived in Laguna Beach, California, in a very funky house, perched high above the Pacific Ocean, with a view that stretched all the way from the Palos Verdes peninsula in the north down to San Diego in the south. Easter was going to be in mid-April this year, and the weather was shaping up to be spectacular.

This was Laguna Beach back in the mid-1970s, before the real estate explosion and the skyrocketing housing prices changed Laguna from a sleepy little beach village to a trendy *destination*. Artists could still afford to live and work here then. The Renaissance Bakery still served its famous hearty borscht. And people would breakfast from eight thirty till eleven, leisurely reading newspapers, and chatting over numerous cups of coffee. Eschbach's was a downtown flower shop in a faux gnome castle with towers, turrets, and a stunning Christmas display each year. People lined up outside the shop and were willing to pay fifty cents just to get inside and browse the multitude of decorated Christmas trees and do a bit of shopping. There were no T-shirt or frozen yogurt shops back then, and there were actually times when the beaches would be virtually empty on weekdays, even in the summer.

The boys' house had a steep flight of steps that wound up from the street below. There was one very large eucalyptus tree slightly shading part of the house, but the rest of the hillside was devoid of trees and consisted only of rough ground cover barely supported by the poor soil. The house had one large room that stretched across the front, with the exterior walls a constant row of windows to take advantage of the spectacular views. There was a simple kitchen, a bedroom, and a bath at the back of the house. A large deck warped around two sides—one side being the front of the house, and the other along the entrance by the kitchen.

Both Bryce and Delgado were passionate about roses and had managed to enrich a plot of soil, below the deck by the entrance, enough to support a bed of quite hardy rose bushes just now about to burst into their first bloom of the season. They had been watching the buds carefully, with great anticipation, hoping they would bloom by Easter. They wanted to use them to decorate the long table set up on the deck for the dinner.

Just as dusk was descending on this Saturday evening before Easter, Delgado went outside, once again, to check on the roses. He inspected them carefully and was convinced that they would indeed open up into full bloom tomorrow morning. He checked the soil and decided not to water this evening as he did not want to over-water and risk delaying the blooms.

Bryce was busy in the kitchen preparing *ommok houria*, a Tunisian carrot salad, to be served with sliced hard-boiled eggs and pitted Kalamata olives. He had peeled, sliced, and cooked the carrots till they were tender and transferred them to a large bowl. He minced flat leaf parsley and added that. He finished it off with caraway seeds, olive oil, red wine vinegar, salt, pepper, and a wonderful Moroccan spice paste called harissa. He mixed this well and covered the bowl and let it rest at room temperature overnight. He would add the eggs and olives when he prepared the platter tomorrow just before serving.

☆☆☆

Sandra, an expansive lady in her early sixties, lived just down the coast from the boys. She lived perched in a tower over the ocean with the waves constantly crashing beneath her. Her apartment was part of a large, early twentieth century estate that spread across the cliffs above a private beach. The estate had been subdivided into apartments of various sizes, and Sandra had been living in her small tower for several years.

She dressed mostly in beige and black, with large hats, flowing scarves and bold contemporary jewelry; and as she was a tall woman, she could carry off the most stunning outfits with great aplomb. She had excellent and expensive tastes, and a large portion of her income as an architect went into her extensive wardrobe.

Sandra loved Easter and had been coloring eggs for several days. She planned to go early to the party and, with Bryce's help, hide the eggs around the property for the hunt after dinner. She had a gold egg and a silver egg that represented first and second prize for whoever found them. She had neatly wrapped gifts in colorful Easter paper for the prizewinners. She also had chocolate eggs, marshmallow bunnies with pink ears, and marzipan eggs wrapped in brightly colored foil.

Now Sandra knew that the theme of this Easter was to be a Moroccan feast but her culinary talents did not stretch too much further than her hard-boiled Easter eggs. However, her one surefire dinner contribution and crowd pleaser was the always stunning canned green beans in mushroom soup, garnished with a can of French fried onions. Well, it was almost Moroccan. After all, France *had* occupied Morocco for many years. Certainly by now her green bean recipe must be a Moroccan staple. All she would need to do tomorrow morning would be to heat it through in the oven just before she left for the party.

✩✩✩

Butch and Eva had known Bryce and Delgado from their New York City days. Eva was also from Argentina and had known Delgado when they were both dancers in Buenos Aires. Butch had been a taxi driver in Manhattan, though she was from Brooklyn. Butch and Eva had been a couple for almost ten years now. Bryce and Delgado had been together for four years.

Butch was New York Irish-Italian. She could make a great Italian braciole (her aunt's recipe), an Argentine asado (thanks to her time in Argentina with Eva), or a bang-up Irish corned beef and cabbage dinner—her dad loved it. Today she was making baklava with wildflower honey. This might be considered more Greek than Moroccan, but who cared, Butch figured.

Eva was nagging on about how she wanted the kitchen cabinets painted and waved paint samples at Butch as she was trying to cook. Butch was just finishing up the syrup for the desert—a cup and a half of wildflower honey, a half-cup of water, a tablespoon of lemon juice, three cloves and a cinnamon stick. She had boiled the ingredients and was checking the temperature with a candy thermometer for a 230° reading.

"What do you think about the Adriatic Yellow?" Eva asked, holding up the paint sample against the side of the cabinet by the kitchen window.

"Love ya to pieces," Butch declared, as she removed the solid ingredients from the syrup. "But this is *not* a good time for me to be discussing paint colors. Do you think you could give me a helping hand instead?"

"Oh jeeze," Eva replied, "what ya need?"

"Could you please check the phyllo dough and see if it's okay? Gotta keep it moist."

Eva peeked under the damp towel and gently fingered the dough. It was fine. "Just dandy."

"Good. Now hand me the filling."

Eva handed her the bowl—two thirds cup of pistachios, one half cup of almonds and one third cup of walnuts, all coarsely chopped with a quarter cup of sugar and cinnamon, cardamom, and a touch of salt. Butch had also added a couple of secret ingredients of her own—some orange and lemon zest and a moistening of cognac.

"Thanks. Gotta work quickly now so the dough doesn't dry out," Butch commented and then proceeded to line a buttered baking dish with a leaf of the phyllo dough before brushing it with melted butter. She repeated this with another leaf till she had a layer of six. She was using so much butter you would have thought that she had a cow parked outside the back door. She covered the remaining dough with the moist towel and reached for the bowl with the filling. She spread a third of the filling over the dough in the baking dish and repeated this two more times with the dough and the filling. She then cut the baklava into diamond shapes and shoved it into a 400° oven till crisp and brown— about 35 minutes.

When it was done, she pulled it out, put it on a rack to cool and then carefully poured the honeyed syrup over the entire pan, letting it soak into the cooling pastry.

"Damn, you're good." Eva leaned over and kissed the back of Butch's neck. "Can I have a piece?" She reached over and picked at the edge of the sweet temptation.

Butch slapped her hand. "Bryce would skin me alive if I came to the party with a piece missing. You're just going to have to wait."

"Awww." Eva sulked and smacked Butch back with a paint sample.

☆☆☆

George lived in a fantasy house on a cliff right above the ocean. His house looked like a French half-timber manor with a Norman tower that descended to the beach via a spiral staircase. George had been a Hollywood cinematographer for many years but escaped from the rat race to retire to his retreat where he puttered and lovingly restored his dream house over several years.

George had a houseguest this weekend. Samantha was a British lady of some years (she would never reveal her true age) who resided in New York City and would visit for several weeks at a time. They had met many years ago on the beaches of Mexico and had kept up a scintillating

61

friendship ever since.

George was adept at salads and simple breakfasts involving smoked salmon but had absolutely no idea how to approach a Moroccan feast. On this Saturday morning, he was plowing through a Mediterranean cookbook someone had given him one Christmas because "the pictures were so nice." He was mumbling and cursing and swatting at pages looking for something suitable—and easy. Samantha came to the rescue.

"I can't believe you have no idea how to cook at your advanced age," she taunted as she pulled the book from him and turned smartly to the index. She studied the entries under Morocco and pointed. "Here, just the thing," she pronounced as she selected a *tagine batata hloowa,* pointing to the entry like she was instructing a toddler in calculus.

George stared at her as though she had just given birth to a calf. "I have no idea what that is."

"Of course not, you're an infidel." She pointed to the top of a kitchen cabinet where he had a fancy array of culinary pottery displayed—all for decoration, probably covered in dust, and, without a doubt, never used. "And what do you suppose that is?" she asked in a very superior mode, pointing to a rough looking dish with a tall conical lid.

"A dish," he replied, not about to let her snippy attitude intimidate him.

"It's a tagine," she smirked. "A Moroccan baking dish."

"Well, goodie. Looks like it will hold a dandy salad."

"Oh..." She brushed him aside and started rummaging through his cupboards and refrigerator. "Get it down."

"Please?" he taunted.

"Yes. Please." She looked at it as he brought it down. "And clean it up while you're at it."

As he was washing the tagine, she pulled out several cans of pearl onions left over from some Christmas long ago, some yams, some carrots, and a bag of somewhat dried-out pitted prunes. "Do you have any sesame seeds?" she asked, fishing through a cupboard of spices and pulling out what else she would need to season the dish.

"What are *they*?"

"Useless, useless," she mumbled, finally finding a small packet at the back of the spice shelf. "Good, this will work out nicely."

"Need any help?" he asked, indeed, beginning to feel useless.

She looked around at what she had gathered. "Yes, can you peel the yams? You do have a peeler somewhere, yes?"

He rummaged in a drawer and pulled out a splendid peeler, presenting it to her as if he had just brought home the Heisman Trophy.

"Excellent."

He continued to hold it up, quite unaware of what to do with it.

"So peel the yams," she nudged.

"Oh, yeah." He turned to the sink and set to work.

Samantha sautéed the pearl onions in a pan with some butter. She took out half and placed them aside. George had finished peeling the yams.

"Here, peel and slice these," she directed, giving George several carrots. She cubed the yams and placed them in the sauté pan with the remaining onions. She added the carrots when George was done, cooking them till they were slightly browned. She added two cups of vegetable broth, a quarter cup of honey, some cinnamon, ground ginger, a cup of the pitted and chopped prunes and some salt and pepper. She placed the entire mixture into the bottom of the tagine, covered it with the lid, and put it into a 400° oven and baked it till the vegetables were tender. When she lifted off the tagine lid, the most delicate and intoxicating aromas filled the kitchen. Samantha added the reserved onions and cooked the tagine for five minutes more. She had toasted the sesame seeds and kept them aside to sprinkle over the tagine just before serving.

George commented as she took the tagine out of the oven for the last time, "Wow that smells pretty damn good."

Samantha nodded and acknowledged the obvious. "Of course."

Delgado was up early Easter morning, basting the lamb once again with the marinade before it would go on the grill. He was an early riser and almost always preceded Bryce to the shower. He puttered in the kitchen, making coffee, and feeding the cat. He snacked on some leftover pizza from the night before and then, with great anticipation, stepped outside to check the roses. He stood on the deck, greeted the sun, just now crowning the hill behind the house, and stretched. He walked down to the rose bushes to inspect the blooms and was in complete shock when he saw that all the buds were nipped off cleanly at the stem. He let out a cry and raced back into the house, through to the bedroom. He threw himself on top of Bryce soundly asleep, snuggled up in the bed. Bryce scrambled awake and sat up with a shock.

"What?"

"The deer! They've gotten all the roses."

"What?" He could hardly focus, let alone comprehend what Delgado was saying.

"Our roses. Gone."

Bryce was still not getting it. "You got roses?"

"No. The deer. They...have...eaten...all...the...roses."

Now Bryce got it. He leaped out of bed, rushed stark naked outside, and dashed down to the rose bed. He examined the truncated bushes. "What makes you think it was deer?"

"Do you know of any rose burglars out and about?" Delgado snidely remarked. He stared at Bryce. "Will you please come inside? We don't need to have you arrested for indecent exposure on Easter morning."

"But our roses. They were just *perfect*. What are we going to do for the table? I didn't get any other flowers because we had *these*." Bryce stumbled back into the house, stubbing his toe on the steps to the deck, mumbling and cursing.

☆☆☆

Dan and Virginia, a couple now in their early forties, had spent ten years in Iran, teaching music and theatre. This was long before the revolution, and they had been favored by the Shah and his Queen in their educational endeavors.

Though it was not quite Moroccan, they were going to prepare a delicious crispy rice dish—a favorite from their Iranian days.

Virginia came in from the garden with an armful of freshly clipped iris in a variety of soft pastel colors to take to the party. She knew how much Bryce and Delgado loved to decorate the table for their famous feasts. Dan was working away on the rice dish. Virginia placed the blooms in water till it was time to leave for the party just before noon.

Dan had washed three cups of rice, picked over and cooked a cup and a half of lentils for ten minutes and drained them. He was now sautéing one onion, thinly sliced, in oil. He added a cup of raisins, two cups of pitted chopped dates, and two tablespoons of slivered, candied orange peel, mixing well and setting the mixture aside.

"What is this?" Virginia asked with a laugh as she came back into the kitchen from the bedroom.

"Oh my god, that's Drippy. I'd completely forgotten I still had that," Dan explained. "Where'd you find it?"

"At the bottom of your sock drawer."

"Snooping for dirty secrets, huh?" he joked.

"No-o-o-o. Was putting your laundry away, Mr. Smart Stuff."

Virginia closely examined Drippy. It was a yellow sponge rubber ring about the size of a fifty-cent piece with a component of faux paste flowers at the top. "A bit small for a sex toy," she commented.

Dan laughed. "Well yes, as you know, I would need something considerably larger."

"You are so bad."

Dan continued working on the rice. He had cooked and drained three cups of long grain basmati rice and rinsed it several times. In the pot he had used to cook the rice, he poured half a cup of melted clarified butter.

"And exactly what is—and how do you happen to have—this Drippy?" Virginia continued, pressing forward with her enquiry.

Dan placed two large serving spoons of rice, two tablespoons of yogurt, and a few drops of one teaspoon of ground saffron dissolved into four tablespoons of hot water in the pot with the butter. He spread this mixture over the bottom of the pan. This would help create a golden crust.

"Well, many Christmases ago when I was just a lad, my family got this arcane object as a present from my grandparents. Its intended use was a complete mystery to all of us. You can imagine the speculation as to its use or abuse. It became such a hit that it was given back and forth as a joke present over many seasons. I can't remember how, but at some point we delicately asked the grandparents what it was for, not wanting to offend them, of course, by not knowing its use. Well, it turns out that it was meant to be placed over the spout of a teapot to catch drips—and was thus christened Drippy. Somehow over the years I ended up with it and it migrated to my sock drawer and was forgotten till some daring archeologist rediscovered it in the Temple of Sock."

Dan put two more heaping spoons of rice in the pot. He had a mix of cinnamon, cardamom, cumin, and ground rose petals. He sprinkled half the mixture over the rice. He added a spoonful of lentils, some of the raisin mixture, and then more rice—repeating the layering till it was all in the pot. He then sprinkled the rest of the spice mixture over the pyramid of rice and fruit. He covered the pot and cooked it for ten minutes more over medium heat.

"Well, what would you think if I wrapped up Drippy and we gave it to the boys and let them see if they can figure out what it is? Unless, of course, it is an ancestral treasure by now that must not be parted with."

"No, that's a great idea. Do you mind wrapping it? I'm kinda tied up with this right now."

"Sure." She disappeared.

After ten minutes of cooking the rice, Dan poured a mixture of one more half cup of clarified butter with a half cup of water over the rice mixture. He then poured the remaining saffron water over it as well. He placed a towel over the pot and covered that firmly with the pot lid. It continued to cook over low heat for fifty minutes more.

Virginia came back with a small, beautifully wrapped gift. "I found an old ring box. I think it will make the perfect presentation for Drippy, don't you think?"

Dan smiled. "Splendid." He removed the pot from the stove and let it cool covered for five minutes. This would help free the crust from the bottom of the pot. He would serve the rice when they arrived at the party, detaching the crusty rice from the bottom and serving it around the mound of softer rice.

☆☆☆

Alain and Robert were to drive down to Laguna Beach from Los Angeles. Alain had been Bryce's lover many years ago when Bryce had worked in Cameroon in the Peace Corps and Alain, who was French, had been there as a member of Doctors Without Borders. Alain had settled in Los Angeles at a prestigious research institute. He had met the younger Robert, who had been his waiter at L'Orangerie, one fateful evening. They had become a couple soon after. Bryce and Alain had remained good friends—but much more like family, really.

Alain and Robert, neither particularly adept at cooking, had concocted an appetizer tray of pita, hummus, Kalamata olives, sliced cucumber, and cubes of feta cheese.

"You're not going to wear *that*?" Alain queried, looking askance at the bright purple shirt Robert was putting on.

"What's wrong with it? It's Easter," Robert responded. "I think it's nice and colorful."

"*Oh please*, go as a bunny if you like, but please spare us *that*. You look like a pregnant Easter egg."

"And how exactly can an Easter egg be pregnant, if you please? An egg is already pregnant. How can it be pregnant, pregnant?"

Alain waved this comment away.

"I suppose you're concerned what Bryce will think of me," Robert poked back.

"Oh Robert," Alain said dismissively. "Don't give me that 'jealous of Bryce' routine again. You *know* that was a gazillion years ago. I only have undying affection for your sweet little ass. You know that." He swatted Robert on the behind with his towel. "Here, try this on." Alain handed Robert a stunning sunny yellow silk shirt from his side of the closet.

"Oooo, very nice." Robert took the shirt and sensually slipped it on. "Mine to keep?"

"Not on your life." Alain chose a deep blood red silk shirt for himself and started to put it on.

"Oh, you're not going to wear *that*, are you?" Robert added, looking at Alain with a wry smile.

67

They left at ten thirty in order to arrive in Laguna by noon.

☆ ☆ ☆

Bryce was in charge of tending to the charcoal grill and was letting the briquettes reach temperature before Delgado put on the lamb. It was just a little after eleven, and Bryce and Delgado could hear Sandra calling from the street below. She was the first guest to arrive and was calling for some help in bringing up her dozens of eggs, prizes, and of course the famous green bean casserole. Bryce hurried down the steps to help.

"You have to help me hide these," Sandra said, indicating the cartons of colored eggs. "We have to get them all hidden before the others get here."

"Of course," Bryce offered. "Oh your green bean casserole." He peered into one of the shopping bags, not quite able to mask his disappointment. "You *do* know the theme of this party is Morocco."

"Oh, I know. But everybody would be so disappointed if I didn't bring this. You can't mess with tradition."

"I guess."

They finally reached the summit, and Bryce helped Sandra with her various bags and bundles. She immediately began issuing orders once she had greeted, embraced, and kissed Delgado on both cheeks. "Is the white wine nice and cold?" she hinted.

"Oh, yes. You ready?" Delgado asked.

She looked at him as if he had just escaped from the rubber room.

"I'll bring it right over." Delgado smartly poured her a glass.

She turned back to Bryce. "Now, these are the marzipan eggs. We should mix them up with the regular ones and these chocolate eggs in the foil. I'll put the prizes over here. Aren't they nicely wrapped? I just love the little chickies on this paper, don't you?"

"Ah..." Bryce tried to answer but was cut off.

"If you'll just take these, then, we can get them all securely hidden. Do you like my hat? It's new."

"Ravishing."

Delgado brought the wine to Sandra. "How's the grill?" Delgado asked Bryce, trying to rescue him.

"Let's just go check."

The two of them escaped to the deck.

"Be right back." Bryce waved to Sandra and, giggling, the two rushed to the grill to check on the coals.

"I'll just get the eggs out of the bags. Don't be long," Sandra sang out.

"I still have to make the yogurt sauce," Bryce said to Delgado as he poked at the glowing coals.

"The coals are just about ready," Delgado added. "Shall I put the lamb on yet? What do ya think?"

"How long does it take?"

"I'm thinking about forty-five minutes to an hour."

Bryce checked his watch. It was now eleven thirty. "No one's ever on time. We don't want it overcooked. Let's wait till twelve."

They started back toward the entrance to the house. As they passed the already set table, Bryce sadly noticed the lack of roses.

"Hey guys," Margot called out to the boys as she appeared at the top of the steps, all flounces, lace, and a tie-dyed shawl, her arms filled with bunches of flowers and a grocery flat laden with an assortment of luscious looking fruits.

"Margot!" Delgado shouted out as he came forward, taking the flat of fruit and giving her a big kiss on the cheek. "Look at you, all dressed up in your Easter drag." Delgado turned to Bryce. "Here are the flowers for your table after all."

"Great."

Margot was an aerobics instructor at a very exclusive residential spa in Topanga Canyon. She was trim and saucy in a very California blonde kind of way.

"Man, these look fantastic," Bryce commented, poking at the fruit in the flat. "Are these from Gypsy Boots?" He referred to a natural grocery known for its superior fruits and vegetables.

"Oh yeah. And if you like, I'll put together a fruit salad. Not very Moroccan, I guess, but hey, fruit is universal, no?" Margot spotted Sandra and rushed over to give her a big hug. "Don't you look fantastic!"

Margot commented to Sandra.

"You like my new hat?"

Margot belted out a laugh. "You are too funny."

Sandra was a little hurt. "Don't you like it?"

"Oh I love it. Love you. Just glad to see you."

"Glass of wine?" Delgado offered.

"Natch." Margot took the offering and laughed again.

Sandra pulled at Bryce's sleeve. "The eggs..."

"Oh yeah."

Just then Samantha appeared, tagine in hand, followed by George, lagging behind as he ascended the last of the steps. He was not in the best of shape.

"George was hopeless at anything Moroccan, so I put together this nice little vegetarian tagine for the dinner," Samantha offered.

"Splendid." Delgado accepted the tagine. "Does it need to be heated?"

"That would be great. Then I have to sprinkle these on top," she added, shaking the packet of toasted sesame seeds.

George came forward with a couple of bottles of wine. "Hi all, Sandra, Margot." He nodded.

Bryce whispered to Delgado. "I've got to make the yogurt sauce. I think you can put the lamb on now if you like." Delgado nodded and took the lamb out of the refrigerator.

"Bryce, the eggs." Sandra tried reaching Bryce with her urgency.

"Be right there. Just need to make this first," he called back. He was concocting a sauce to serve with the lamb. It consisted of Greek yogurt, minced garlic, shredded cucumber, freshly chopped mint from the garden, and lemon juice. Delgado, having put the lamb on the grill, was passing out more glasses of wine. Samantha had gone up to Sandra and was commenting on her new hat. Sandra momentarily forgot about the eggs.

Butch and Eva poked their way into the kitchen, bearing the baklava.

"Here, take a whiff of this." Butch offered Bryce as he was grating a cucumber.

"Wow! Do we need to heat that up later?"

"No, it's better at room temp."

Eva was chatting with Margot and George.

Dan and Virginia and Robert and Alain all arrived at the same time. Delgado's lamb on the grill sent clouds of smoke from the olive oil and lamb juices wafting toward the crowd. Delgado raced over to turn the lamb and damped down the flames with a spray bottle of water.

"Do you have a serving platter I can use?" Dan asked Bryce, as he was finishing up the sauce.

"Ah yeah, right up there." Bryce pointed to the top of a kitchen cabinet.

"Hi, sexy." Alain leaned in and gave Bryce a kiss.

"Hey, guy, you made it. Great. Robert here?"

"Of course. He's setting out the appetizers. Brought some wine as well," Alain added.

"Great. There's some more over there. Help yourselves."

Bryce was frantically trying to make some table decorations with the flowers that Margot and Virginia had brought when Sandra came over.

"The eggs," Sandra commanded.

Bryce looked up. "Could you find someone else to help, my dear? I'm just swamped here."

Margot leaned in. "Do you have a paring knife for the fruit?"

"In that drawer," he indicated.

Dan was plating piles of rice next to Bryce at the counter. Samantha was placing the tagine into the oven on the other side. Margot was slicing fruit. Delgado suddenly appeared behind Bryce and put his arms around his waist and laid his head against Bryce's shoulder.

"Hey, honey, would you like a glass of wine?"

"I'd love one," he sighed.

☆☆☆

Sandra had finally found a willing soul to help her hide the eggs. Robert had gladly obliged. Actually, Robert did most of the hiding with Sandra pointing to exactly where she wanted each treasure hidden.

The lamb was perfectly pink. The green bean casserole was lavishly praised, although somewhat passed over. The crispy Persian rice was a delight. The delicate vegetarian tagine was succulent. And the honeyed baklava was the perfect ending to the meal, accompanied by mounds of fruit salad.

Sandra orchestrated the Easter egg hunt and awarded the prizes to the lucky finders of the gold and silver eggs. The wine was liberally consumed. And after several rounds of Fictionary, several hands of bridge for the card players in the group, and lengthy spirited conversations leaning on the deck railings watching the sun sink behind Catalina, the guests finally gathered their platters, bowls, and tagine and disappeared into the rosy dusk after a most successful and appreciated feast.

Dan, Virginia, and Margot had lingered behind to help with clearing the table and the washing up. Margot left directly after, as she had a long drive back to the spa.

Bryce brought out the cognac and a few candles, and the four of them who were left settled into deck chairs to watch the stars come out and the new crescent moon dip gently into the ocean.

"Dan?" Virginia nudged him and nodded her head. He looked at her, not understanding. "The box," she added.

"Oh yeah, totally forgot." He fished in his jacket and pulled out the little present for the boys. "Here, we found this treasured family heirloom that we thought was totally *you guys*."

Bryce accepted the gift—very obviously a ring box. "Oh wow. Really?" He handed the box to Delgado and let him unwrap it. He tore off the paper and, seeing that it was a ring box, looked at Bryce with some hesitation. Was this going to be some horribly expensive gift that they just could not accept?

"Go ahead. Open it," Dan prompted.

Delgado handed it back to Bryce who snapped open the lid. They both stared in mute bewilderment at Drippy, having no idea whatsoever what it was.

Bryce scrunched up his face and looked at Dan. "Not quite sure what this is exactly. But I like the little floral arrangement on the top. Care to enlighten us as to what this might be?"

Both Dan and Virginia rolled about with laughter.

Finally Dan replied, "Ah, the mysteries of the universe. You have been presented with the immutable Drippy. One of the great secrets of all time and space. It is now in your possession, and it will be up to the two of you to decipher what can be revealed only by the study and practice of the uses and abuses of the revered Drippy."

Both Dan and Virginia lapsed back into a fit of laughing. Bryce and Delgado more closely examined the gift but could not fathom the mystery, so they set it aside for the moment.

They continued to chat softly in the light of the few candles for a while, and then finally Dan and Virginia excused themselves and departed, leaving Bryce and Delgado, exhausted, content, and already halfway dreaming.

The leftovers were neatly wrapped and stored. The bare table on the deck was waiting to be dismantled in the morning and stored until the next great tribal event. The ring box with Drippy silently released its mysterious vibrations into the bedroom from its perch on the boys' dresser. And Bryce and Delgado were snuggled up together with the cat fast asleep in the bed between them, while the deer gently nibbled on the baby beets in the newly sprouting vegetable garden behind the house.

Cry of the Wolf

Note: *I discovered this manuscript during my genealogical research at the Institute Historique Strasbourg in 2003. In the ensuing years, I have worked diligently to carefully translate this manuscript into English. It has been my aim to capture the natural feel of the original manuscript without updating it or making it sound too contemporary. I will leave the final judgment of that to the reader. However, I feel that this document provides a rare glimpse into a life in the fourteenth century, and an examination of a subject little understood or referenced at that time.*

Henry Traubb, Chicago, 2010

Nineteenth of March in the Year of Our Lord 1347

I am Warin, son of Ranulf and Alma of the House of Thann by the town of Arzviller, a day's cart ride from Strasbourg on Rhine. I am writing this because I know not what else to do. The sadness in my heart must find some form of expression, and I may not speak of my story with anyone. I write this for myself alone and pray that it will never be read by another living soul.

It is late at night. I do not have left but a short candle by which to write. It is quiet in the great house, and I can hear only my own breathing, the wind whispering down the chimney, and the cry of the wolf in the far field, or perhaps he's in the nearby Cham Woods. I hear his cry almost every night at this time. He is a lone wolf; his pack long wiped out or moved on. He cries often—hunted, unloved, separated, and no doubt always hungry. He does not seem to wake the neighbors or my

75

family. I alone hear his pain.

I am of two and twenty years. My father is the principal landowner in this county. His serfs raise sheep for wool, and then we weave it in our warehouse and trade it in Strasbourg, shipping it down the river to even greater trade centers.

Our family name is much revered and feared locally. The great Emperor Charlemagne bestowed on our family the crest of Lion Rampant Reguardant above a quadrant shield with two crowns and two fields of stars. My father is very proud of this great honor and finds every occasion to display it prominently.

My mother and my sisters, Nesta and Linota, are modest by comparison to my brash father. They are adept in the womanly arts, and peacefully pursue their quiet lives hidden away from the toils of either village or city life.

My father has engaged me to Celestria of Alcuin, but we have yet to marry at the time this narrative begins. She is dark of hair and pleasing of appearance, and her family's land adjoins ours and will enlarge our domain greatly. That is very pleasing to my father, who dreams of our lands stretching all the way from the far reaches of Lagarde to the edge of Arzviller. I have met her but twice, and she speaks well and is adept at tapestry, I understand. If my report of her seems less than enthusiastic, it is because of what has transpired in my life this past year and is, indeed, the subject of this writing.

To begin, let me reflect upon my character and temperament—if one may be objective about such an examination. I have been told I am comely. I am dark of hair and have eyes of blue, a rarity in this region. I ride well and have learned all the skills necessary to engage in commerce, at my father's insistence. I already manage the warehouse where the wool is prepared and woven into a rough cloth, much desired for its warmth in the mountain regions to the south. I have a slight build and have never excelled at the martial arts, to my father's great disappointment. And though it is a passion with my father, I find the hunting of any animal or bird abhorrent. But it is something I must do, as I am a now a grown man and am expected to contribute game to the family table.

I have a burning passion for books, though they are very rare and difficult to obtain. Our library is scant, but I have been blessed with the opportunity to borrow volumes from the fathers at the monastery in Ascenseur. They are very kind and attentive to me and gladly lend me books for as long as I need them. I sometimes wonder at their kindnesses to me, though. They are so pleased when I visit and seem greatly reluctant to let me part. I am as yet unschooled in many of the ways of the world, but I believe I can detect longing and sadness in their eyes when I finally leave with my saddlebags tightly packed and with the anticipation of many hours of reading pleasure ahead of me.

I have few friends. I was schooled at home. We live far enough from the village so that I grew up with few boys of my age, or of my class, available for friendship. Those that are on our estate are of serf families and are not considered suitable companions for one of my station. My sisters, while friendly, live in a different world altogether, and our paths rarely cross. Nor do we have enough in common on which to base a friendship. And, I am afraid to say, they are rather dull, being interested only in assembling their trousseaus and obtaining a prestigious marriage.

This is how I see myself—neither a hero, nor a villain. My life is regular, for who I am—and untouched by either great joy or great pain. That is until a year ago, February.

And here I am in the depth of night, about to finally commit my story to writing, a lasting history that will forever seal my fate.

I work regularly now, as I have stated, in my family's wool warehouse. It assists my father, and he is pleased with what I have accomplished there, thus far. Besides the keeping of the accounts, I supervise the workers—carding, spinning, and weaving the wool that comes from our lands. I then accompany the carts to Strasbourg and oversee the loading of the merchandise onto the barges headed to southern ports, where it is eventually sold.

Not long after I began working at the warehouse, I found myself in need of an assistant. Most of our workers are dull and listless, needing constant prodding and oversight, and I despaired of finding a suitable candidate from among our most uninspiring dullards. However, one lad caught my eye. His name is Sevaric and about the same age as I. He is the son of one of our serfs; a good, industrious family, and well respected by my father.

Sevaric works with the raw wool and applies himself with dedication and principle. He is fair of hair—his family being from the north. He is well formed and strong—much stronger than I. I have seen him often staring at me with a longing that I knew signaled a desire for more accomplishment than his restricted life has offered him thus far. He has a sparkle in his eye that shows intelligence and a drive to excel.

One morning, I stood watching him, unseen, as he manipulated the sacks of raw wool, preparing them for carding. He easily hoisted the sacks onto his strong shoulders and moved them adroitly into the next room. Upon his return, he spotted me and stopped, looking at me with his sharp hazel eyes. He smiled and then moved on to the next sack to be moved.

I called out to him, "Sevaric."

"Sir?" He stopped with a load on his shoulders.

"Come to the counting chamber when you have disposed of that," I commanded, with perhaps too strong a demand.

"Sir," he answered briskly, and disappeared into the carding room.

I returned to my chamber and awaited his appearance. Duly he arrived and entered, holding his grubby hat in his hands, wringing it with some anxiety. He stood quietly in front of me, waiting for me to speak first, unsure as to the nature of my summons.

"You may sit if you like," I stated, indicating a chair across from my writing table.

He smiled with some relief and pulled up the chair so he was close by me. I could smell the strong odor of raw wool and sweat emanating from his course shirt. He looked at me with great focus and intensity. I studied him for a moment. I felt very strongly that I had been correct in my assessment of his abilities.

"Sevaric, I have been watching your work here and have been very pleased with what I have seen."

He regarded me with a slight smile and a nod and waited, not responding otherwise.

"Let me ask you a question. Have you had any schooling?"

"Yes, sir. My mother is from a good family up north, and she has had a fair amount of learning and taught me both reading and writing. Also some music."

"Music?"

"I can read music, and I can play the cittern."

I nodded, wondering why I had not noticed this man before now. "I am impressed. Then why are you working here in this laborious position?"

"Sir, it is what my family does. Where else could I go? I am not a gentleman like yourself."

"Can you copy this out for me?" I handed him a page of accounts.

He studied it a moment and answered. "Sir, this is mostly numbers. Are you sure this is what you want me to copy? I can read and copy full pages of text as well."

"Yes, for now, just do that for me."

He proceeded to copy the page, seated at the edge of my table across from me; handing it to me, completed in a fine hand, when he was finished.

"Now, read this." I handed him a book on loan from the fathers.

He took it and read flawlessly. He looked up at me when he had finished the first page. "More?" he asked.

"Not necessary." He handed the book back to me. "Now, a question for you." I hesitated a moment, enjoying creating a little suspense for Sevaric as he waited for my proposal. "I am very impressed with your accomplishments. And you seem to be a very engaging and bright young man. I very much need some assistance with my work both in this counting room and on the floor, and I would like you to assist me."

Sevaric smiled but did not give into any overt emotion. "Will there be a pay increase?" he finally asked.

I held my official face, but a slight twinkle in my eyes gave me away. "Yes, that is very likely."

"And, sir, do you think it possible I might be able to borrow some books from you on occasion? I very much hunger to read more, but books are generally not available to me."

This was a moment of great happiness for me. I had found not only a capable assistant, but I believed I had found a new friend as well.

☆☆☆

Twentieth of March 1347

Again, it is late at night. And though I fear I may suffer from lack of sleep tomorrow, I am once again drawn to continue my narration. Tonight it is almost warm, and I have my casement open to the night breeze.

I have not heard my wolf tonight. Perhaps he has found some peace. I hope it is not because he has encountered a farmer's trap and is no longer with us. I should miss his friendship greatly, as I do believe he knows of me as I know of him.

I shall now continue my story.

The taking on of Sevaric as my assistant proved to be a wise decision. He learned quickly and became an adept companion both at the warehouse and on the outside as well, as he was an expert hunter and would accompany me on my painful expeditions to find game for both his table and mine. Not that I ever grew to enjoy this sport, but I did look forward to our adventures together, where we would talk of music and books and the differences in our lives, while we scouted for game in the hills of our estate. Though, because I was his master, I always had to take the lead in our conversations—much to my sadness, as I always enjoyed hearing his unbridled and spontaneous thoughts when they would break through with his unguarded enthusiasm.

I am reminded of one occasion in particular. We had just come up empty-handed after a brace of quail escaped our capture, and our traps were empty. The day was hot as it was now mid-June. We sought the comfort of shade and the cooling influence of a small natural pond secluded deep in the woods.

I lay down on the bank by the water. A willow hung overhead, and the branches barely swayed because of the stifling heat and the stillness of the air. Sevaric lay down beside me. While I was on my back, staring up at the interior of the willow, he lay on his side, his head supported by his arm, and he looked at me deeply and with a strange expression. A leaf fluttered down from the tree above and landed on my forehead. I was too lazy even to turn my head to dislodge it. Sevaric reached over with his free hand and gently brushed it away. I turned to look at him. Our eyes met and he smiled very slightly.

"How about a swim?" he asked, as he rose and began to undress.

I, being extremely shy about my slight build, and not an accomplished swimmer, declined, but sat up and watched as he undressed. His body was strong and firm, excellently well proportioned, and he gleefully ran toward the water and plunged in. His head emerging from the depths, he shook it like a wet spaniel, his longish blond hair swirling off a glistening spray. He laughed and played, crossing the pond several times with a strong swimmer's stroke. He called out to me.

"You should really come in. It is very cooling in this heat. Just a little way if you are afraid," he taunted, almost daring me.

I stood up, walked to the edge of the pond, and crouched down and put my hand in the water. Even that slight contact was refreshing. The grasses at the edge bent down into the water, inviting me to just slip in. However, there was something else going on with me that prevented me from moving forward. While I had greatly appreciated Sevaric's company for some time now, I also was beginning to recognize a new feeling that was unfamiliar and a bit disturbing. I could not take my eyes off his body gliding through the water like a beguiling serpent. I felt a stirring in my—I am reluctant to utter the word but shall use the common term I have heard on occasion from the workers in the warehouse—cock.

I did not understand this phenomenon as I believe this is a response that is reserved for one's wife. I have little knowledge of these things as I have had very little education about such matters. However, my father has promised me a talk before my marriage with Celestria. Not that I have not relieved myself many times, alone in my bed in the mornings when I would awake with my member stiff and aching for release. I understood this. But this was happening to me now as I watched Sevaric, so graceful, strong, and gleaming in the water. This could not be right. Though I have had some such inklings before when I would come upon a groom nearly naked in the barn on a hot day, tending to our horses. Those stirrings I dismissed as flushes caused by the heat and lack of appropriate exercise. But this today was something else. This had been building in me throughout the day. Besides the great pleasure I derived from Sevaric's company, I was aware that I wanted to be physically near him as well. I would position myself so that our shoulders would touch, or I would brush his hand as we examined a trap together. I remembered the look in his eyes, just now, as we relaxed beneath the tree, and I have no idea what that look signified.

Just then, Sevaric swam over to me at the edge of the pond. He put his hands on the bank, on either side of where I was still crouching. I could not stand up because of my state of arousal, which would surely show. He did not speak, but just looked up at me, again with that mischievous smile—his eyes burning into my depths, throwing me into further confusion. I could not speak, either. He playfully splashed some water at me and laughed, leaning back and pushing off from the shore with the force of his strong legs. I could see that he too had the same problem as I.

I quickly stood and turned away so he could not see my condition. I called out to him, "I think we'd better go now. We need to find some game before we return, or both our families will be displeased."

He forcefully swam to the shore and pulled himself out of the water, still in an aroused condition, but he did not seem to mind or be embarrassed by it in any way. He quickly dried himself with his shirt, dressed, and presented himself to me ready to continue the hunt.

☆☆☆

Second of April 1347

It has been difficult for me to come back to this correspondence, as what I am now to recite pains me, and I have a great deal of guilt about what is to follow.

I am afraid that as a result of my discoveries about myself that day at the pond, I have behaved badly. Instead of finding some way to punish my own wayward flesh, I turned my confusion and inner torment into a desire to punish Sevaric. I became very cold to him at the warehouse. I refused his entreaties to accompany me hunting—and was especially adamant about avoiding swims—and I harshly refused to lend him any of my books. He took it very badly. While he would never utter a word of protest or reproach me in any way, I could see the pain and bewilderment in his eyes—those beautiful hazel eyes.

I foolishly urged my father to hasten the wedding, and he was greatly pleased with that, and arranged an engagement banquet for the next month. It was to be a grand affair in the fullness of summer. The house was in constant activity as my father was hosting many of the finest families in the district. The kitchen was bursting with game, slaughtered domestic animals, great cakes, pies both sweet and savory, and mounds of fruits and vegetables fresh from our orchards and gardens. My sisters were recruited to fashion masses of garlands for both interior and exterior decoration. It took two days for the servants to prepare the dining hall. Again, an abundance of flowers graced the tables, and there was a bevy of servants carefully measuring each place setting and amassing an army of candles.

My father engaged the very best tailor of the district to fashion new attire for the entire family; all of us fitted out most elegantly, befitting our wealth and station.

I, by this time, was embroiled in many conflicting emotions. I was disgusted by what I considered to be the excesses of this pending event. I realized that I had been rash in persuading my father to push ahead with the wedding and was dreading having to spend so much time and attention on Celestria, who would be increasingly in my company after the engagement. It was beginning to dawn on me that I would be marrying her in October, and I would be forever linked to her and cut off from so many of my solitary freedoms and joys.

And my self-isolation from Sevaric was a new and growing pain. With all the constant activity and duties surrounding the impending banquet, I had barely attended to my work at the warehouse, which accorded, however, with my father's wishes. It wasn't until the day of the event itself that I was to learn that Sevaric was to personally serve Celestria and me at the banquet supper. My father had recognized the same qualities in Sevaric that I had and persuaded him to serve us, thinking it would be a compliment to me as I had discovered and promoted him. But for me it was both a great pain and a great joy. I was racked with guilt over my treatment of him and found, that instead of my feelings abating, they were enflamed by our separation. I would toss in my bed at night, haunted by the image of him emerging from the pond—golden, wet, erect.

The day before the banquet, tormented and unsettled, I took my horse and rode off by myself into the woods without telling anyone where I was going. I returned to our pond, and throwing myself on the bank where we had lain, wept—letting out a cry that I prayed would be heard by no one. I actually cried myself into a slumber and awoke just before dusk, knowing I would be missed at the house and would incur my father's wrath when I returned.

As I awoke, I sensed a presence across the pond. I had slept deeply in my grief and had a difficult time focusing in the dusk. I lifted myself into a seated position and stared across the water. There on the far bank was a wolf. He stared at me for a long time and then raised his head and let out a howl and finally turned and disappeared into the darkness of the surrounding woods. I would grow to know that cry. I would hear it many nights in the solitude of my chamber. His cry would later become my cry.

Seventh of April 1347

I have been absent from my recitation for a week. The pain of looking at these shortcomings of mine has prevented me from returning until now. But I feel an urgency to complete this as events outside of my control may soon interrupt this narrative in ways I cannot now comprehend.

I must, with some anguish, relate the events of the day of the banquet. The morning broke with a splendid sky. A dawn of rose and pale yellow bespoke of happy nuptials—for all but me. I had been soundly scolded for my absence the afternoon and early evening before the banquet. My father's fury was only mitigated by his pleasure in the morrow's events. He quickly dismissed his anger and moved quickly to engage me in a hearty discussion of the joys of matrimony, including the "talk" he had promised me concerning my husbandly duties. I was mortified with embarrassment; and so, as it turned out, was he. The discussion ended up being mercifully brief and somewhat sketchy, lacking in explicit detail.

It had been a long time since the village and district had witnessed such a stunning event as our banquet. Carriages, carts, and horses drew up to our entrance. Our grooms and footmen were frantic, tending to the many arrivals. It could not have been a more perfect day, as a storm had moved through during the previous night, and the morning was clear and cooler than usual, preventing excessive discomfort in our packed dining hall.

I will not dwell on the banquet itself, except to say it was lavish and all that my father had hoped for. My bride-to-be was at my side, and we exchanged minimal conversation as her mother was on my other side and constantly plied me with a running commentary on the event and endless questions about our business and financial success. However, I paid her scant attention as my focus was elsewhere.

Sevaric stood obediently behind me. He was dressed in the household livery. And while he was attentive to Celestria, he was lavish in his attention to me. He refilled my goblet practically after each sip of wine I took. I could not help but notice that each time he leaned forward, he would brush my shoulder, or his hand would lightly touch my neck as he whisked away a fly. Again, I was overcome by the same sensations that had plagued me at the pond the day of his swim. Luckily, I was wearing a jacket that covered the most prominent manifestation of my discomfort. But I could not help but notice that Sevaric suffered the same indignation as me, though he covered it well from all but me to see. A moment came when our eyes met for a brief second. He could not suppress his shy but devastating smile. I became both enflamed and chilled at the same moment. My hand began to shake as I raised the goblet to drink in an attempt to quell my flushes and violent feelings.

85

Celestria noticed my agitation and turned to me.

"Are you well, my beloved?" she asked, placing her delicate hand on my arm.

I looked down at her hand then up into her eyes, which I am sure would enflame many another manly breast. I nodded, for I could not speak just then.

"It may be the heat. I find this hall to be extremely cloistering with this many guests. Will you please excuse me a moment?" I finally asked. She nodded, and as I arose, her mother looked at me with a peculiar expression as I passed behind her.

Sevaric reached out to me as I escaped and asked, "Do you need my assistance, sir?"

I stopped and looked at him. "Not just yet." And I fled out of the hall, my father looking after me with some concern.

I rushed to my chambers and splashed water on my face and the back of my neck and then sat on the edge of my bed and collected my thoughts and my breath, as I had been breathing hard, short pants as I escaped the hall.

Finally, composing myself and shedding some of the heavy outer garments that the formal occasion required, I returned to the banquet hall.

I will not relate the torture of the endless lines of well-wishers I had to endure, nor the agony of the relentless barrage of questioning from the pending in-laws. Just let it be noted that finally the ghastly event ended, and I escaped to my rooms to surrender the formal garments that restricted and enchained me.

I was desperate to escape outside and embrace the cool evening that had finally settled in, relieving me, as a gentle breeze picked up, and I began to, once again, feel a moment of tranquility and peace.

I wandered away from the house, past the barns, with the grooms still active as they put to rest the horses, still skittish from the unusual quartering of the guests' strange mounts in their midst.

I wandered past the house gardens and orchards and into a field of corn, now grown up to the height of my waist. From there I found a sloping bank at the edge of the field covered in an array of wild flowers.

I sat down and watched as the moon rose over the forest across the field. I was very near the edge of tears, once again, as I felt the depth of my sorrow, brought on solely by my own foolish actions. I lay back against the bank, closed my eyes, and contemplated rash actions I might take that would only further enflame my precarious condition. I imagined flight to a foreign realm, sequestration with a sympathetic order of religious devotees, and even, I am ashamed to relate, self-annihilation.

Then, with but the faintest brush of a gentle kiss, I heard whispered in my ear, "Do you need my assistance now, sir?"

I opened my eyes to see Sevaric stretched out beside me. I had not heard, nor sensed, his approach and his reclining down beside me. That is how deeply I was entranced by my own sorrow. I did not react with either shock or fear. I simply stared into his eyes, now clearly visible by the fullness of the moon. His kiss had not only awoken me, but also transformed me. I had crossed a threshold and was no longer a slave to indecision or guilt. I reached over and put my hand softly on his cheek.

"Can you forgive me?" I asked from a heart aching with longing and desire.

He barely stirred. "But there has been no hurt. There is nothing to forgive." He buried his head between my shoulder and my neck and ever so lightly gave me another kiss. I turned toward him, took his head in my hands, and brought him to me, and for the first time in my life, I knew who I was.

☆☆☆

Eighth of May 1347

Again, too long an absence from this discourse. I have read over the preceding lines many times and am astonished at what I have written. Why am I committing this to a hard reality that could be discovered and cause my ruination? I only know I must.

I have been married now since September last. The reason for the earlier date will be explained further along.

My wife is still not pregnant and unlikely to become so. I have refused to perform my marital duties, and my poor desperate wife wildly accuses herself in my failing. How can I begin to console her, for she is such a sweet, innocent, and uncomplicated creature?

I write this in part for her. It is what I would tell her if I could. By writing this, I feel that I am somehow easing her soul, even if she will never know the truth of this story from me in her present life.

I pass now from that night in the field. For me it was the true beginning of my life. My forever hidden life, I believed at that time. Suffice it to say, I discovered that evening what my whole being had been trying to get me to acknowledge for a long time. That day of betrothal to Celestria became, in fact, my night of marriage to Sevaric.

From that time forward, we were nearly inseparable. We had to continue our façade at the warehouse. He was my assistant, and I was his master, but we slipped, without too much discomfort, into our new relationship, masked by the conventions of our stations and work duties. He never questioned our need to conceal our affections.

Though we had consummated our relationship that night in the field, we have never really spent an entire night together in a bed and awoken together the next morning in each other's arms as we both so much longed to do. We have had to be satisfied, instead, with our tenuous encounters in the fields or woods, far from prying eyes. Happy though these moments were, we both still longed for our own privacy and a deeper, more prolonged and intimate connection.

But an opportunity would soon present itself, which we could not then anticipate with greater joy. It was time for me to travel once again to Strasbourg with our latest shipment of merchandise and a final destination down river on the barges. And I, of course, would need my assistant.

Our journey would comprise a full day's journey to Strasbourg, an additional day of negotiation and unloading the shipment, and a third day's return home. That meant two nights together at the inn. It is not uncommon for two men to share a room while traveling, even sharing the same bed, as lodging is scarce and beds even scarcer. You cannot imagine how eagerly we looked forward to that trip.

But as our journey was still several weeks away, we wanted to find agreeable activities to pass the remaining time. Sevaric's enthusiasms were almost like those of a child, and he insisted that I be presented to his family, even though I could not reciprocate by inviting him to meet mine.

"Please," he pleaded one evening as we left the warehouse and walked together toward our homes.

"But how would it look?" I asked in answer to his invitation.

"But you are my master," he answered. "We can make up some reason for you to visit. It would not be untoward for you to call at your serf's house. We can say you have come for an inspection of the property—for tax purposes, let's say. Then it would be only hospitable to offer you some refreshment. You could stay and enter into conversation and before long I could bring out the instruments, and my mother and I could perform for you. Before you knew it, we would have spent a whole evening together. What do you say?"

I nodded my head in thought. How I longed for us to be open together. And how greatly I wished to hold him in front of his family and kiss the back of his neck as I had seen my father do with my mother. "Yes, I think that might be possible," I finally answered. We then walked together in silence, and he dared to take my hand in the gathering dusk.

"Are there others like us?" I asked, unafraid to show my ignorance about such matters.

"There are."

"How do you know? Have you been with a man before me?"

He looked at me, not quite sure how he should answer me, for fear he might upset me.

"I don't mind if you have," I said finally, to ease his hesitation.

"I have," he answered. "But not many. There are places in the village where men can meet. But I have been with no one else since we have been together. Nor do I wish to."

"Where in the village?" I wanted to know as much as I could about who we were.

"Why do you want to know? Want to sample other wares?" he teased, and poked me in the arm.

"Just curious. I know so little."

"Well, there is a place at the edge of the market, not far from the mill. And there is a place under the main bridge out of town, but only at night."

"And you have been to these places?"

He nodded. "But not often."

"Are there many of us?"

"More than you might imagine."

He leaned over and gave me a quick kiss on the cheek as we were now at the point in the road where we had to part for our different ways home. He ran off with a quick look back at me and waved as I stood and watched him till he had completely disappeared.

How greatly we both anticipated our journey to Strasbourg. We would recite the details of the trip together over and over again until the day finally arrived.

Sevaric was early to the warehouse that glorious day. It was now mid-August and it would be hot. We wanted to get an early start, to get as much travel time in as possible while it was still cool in the morning.

When I arrived, he had already bridled the oxen, as the carts had been loaded and prepared for travel the day before. I made a quick inspection of the merchandise, gave final instructions to the supervisor at the warehouse, and we set out—a very respectable looking merchant and his assistant.

We traveled together most of the morning in silence. We each had to attend to the driving of a cart and so were separated and preoccupied with that task. However, we would shout out to each other on occasion, pointing out a feature in the landscape or throwing the water flask between us from cart to cart.

Just before noon, we pulled off the road. Since I had made this trip many times before, I knew of this secluded resting place. A quiet field bordered a sparking stream, rushing briskly toward the Rhine. We uncoupled the oxen and let them drink and graze. I pulled out the basket my mother had prepared for the trip. A gaggle of geese honked across the stream and seemed to protest our intrusion upon their acknowledged terrain. We sought comfort under a tree near the brook, secluded from inspection from the road, and spread out a hearty midday meal before us. Both of us were hungry and quickly satisfied ourselves with my mother's delicious contribution to our journey.

We lay back against the trunk of a large sycamore and closed our eyes briefly, enjoying the peace and the sound of the brook, coolly passing beside us. Sevaric reached over and took my hand. I opened my eyes and turned toward him. His eyes were still closed, but he had a look of such sweet contentment that I could not bring myself to disturb this tranquil moment. Slowly he opened his eyes and turned toward me, and we leaned toward each other and kissed. Little did I know what that kiss would eventually cost us.

I knew that we would have to arrive at the shipping yards in Strasbourg before they were closed and secured for the night. We needed to store our carts and merchandise in the yard for protection. So, after our refreshment, we corralled the oxen, bridled them, and progressed on our way.

The rest of the afternoon was uneventful, but we were spurred on by our desire to reach the city and finally be alone together. We actually arrived a little early, disposed of the carts, secured the oxen for the night, and repaired as quickly as possible to the inn.

By my foresight, I had written to the inn in advance and reserved the very best room for our stay. We decided that during our first evening we would have our dinner in the room and spend the remainder of the evening in each other's arms.

There are some things that I cannot put down in this discourse, even if they will never be read by anyone but me. Events so private and glorious that I cannot find the words to express them, even to myself.

Suffice it to say, that to us, our union was sacred. I am very well aware that this statement is blasphemy in the eyes of the world I live in now. And I am aware that we are threatened with damnation in the eyes of that world. By that world's standards, in the life hereafter, my mind and my soul may be forever in torment; but my body knows differently. Somewhere there is a realm where our love is real, recognized, and honored. I may never find that place, but I know it exists. I will forever celebrate our union, and no man, woman, churchman, lieutenant, officer, or king on high can negate our love. Do what they may; my soul and very being shall ever resist their ignorant tyranny.

Too soon came the end of our business in Strasbourg, and it was time to return home. Sevaric was in the shipping yard bridling the oxen. We had bought provisions to transport home in the empty carts. I slipped away, unseen, for just a moment. There was a silversmith's stall just around the corner. I made a quick purchase and returned before Sevaric even noticed I was gone.

We then proceeded on our journey home and stopped again at the field and brook for our lunch, purchased from the inn. As we sat at the base of the sycamore, having just finished eating, I reached over and took Sevaric's hand. He looked up at me.

I reached into my pocket and took out the two silver rings I had bought from the smith. I didn't say a word but slipped one ring on his finger and then one on mine. He just leaned forward and took me in his arms tears streaming down his face.

"Oh, Warin..." was all he could say.

We separated and looked at each other as we held hands, still seated on the ground.

"I wanted us to wear them now. But when we get back home, they must not be seen." I pulled out two chains. "We must wear them like this." I took off my ring and put it on the chain and then put the chain around my neck and tucked it inside my shirt. "Close to my heart."

He did the same. Then he held his hand over the ring inside his shirt.

"Forever," he said, and we nodded to each other.

☆☆☆

Twelfth of May 1347

News and rumors have been rampant in the county the past few days. It seems that a barge pulled into port in Strasbourg recently, and it is reported that many of the crew were dead or dying from the plague. The ship was immediately quarantined, but that has not quelled the panic, nor stopped the locals from arming themselves to ward off strangers from coming into this area. I am afraid we shall now be entering into a time of even more mistrust and violence.

I feel that I must act quickly to complete this narrative as I do not know if we will have to retire to another part of the country, or even if my own health will be endangered in any way.

To continue the story. My beloved Sevaric and I returned home from our journey to Strasbourg. It had been a very successful venture financially, as we have been promised a handsome price for our goods when they reach their final destination. My father did seem pleased with the results; but surprisingly, he responded with much less enthusiasm than I had anticipated. But for Sevaric and me, the significance of the journey was not in the success of the business, but in the happiness we shared together at the inn.

It was very difficult for Sevaric and me the first few days after our return. We had become accustomed, in just a short while, to express openly our affection for one another and to experience our equality together. So it came as a great shock to be back in the warehouse as master and serf. We were developing, however, a new language of looks and gestures that was known only to us and provided us with some comfort when we were in public together.

Never once were we able to be alone together through an entire night as we had been in Strasbourg, but we were still able to meet secretly, away from our homes or the warehouse. But it would not be too long before autumn and winter would arrive, and we would have to seek more accommodating places to meet than the open countryside.

Then one morning we had an unexpected opportunity to be together again in an intimate way. It was a Sunday and my entire family was off at church. I remained behind, as we were expecting a new horse from Paris, and I was elected to greet the handlers when they arrived.

I was out in the barn overseeing the preparation of a stall for the new stallion, when I spied Sevaric walking through the open field near the spot where we had first united. I called out to him. He saw me and came running over, arriving flushed and breathless. I finished my inspection of the horse accommodations and invited him to follow me, making sure that I was very proper in my relations with him in front of the grooms.

We went into the kitchen, but all of the servants too were at church.

Away from prying eyes, I took him in my arms, and then said, "Come." I lead him up the back stairs to my residential wing, and we secluded ourselves behind my closed and locked door. I knew we only had a brief time together as I could see where the sun touched my writing table and could calculate how far it would travel before my family would return from church.

I flung Sevaric onto my bed and we satisfied ourselves in an almost violent manner, such was our pent-up passion. Lying together after, I gazed into his eyes and put my hand up to his cheek.

"You have not shaved today," I commented, kissing his cheek and feeling the stubble.

"Is it too rough for you?"

I shook my head. "It makes you seem more comely."

"Then I shall never shave again."

I laughed. "No, I would not like you with a full beard, either. You would seem too much like my father, and that would put me off completely," I teased.

He looked at me again without speaking for quite some time and then at last spoke. "Warin, you will be marrying soon." I could see the sadness in his eyes. "What will happen to us then?"

"There will be nothing different for us. For my father the marriage is only about the property he wants to acquire. For me, my marriage has already occurred—that night in the field, and again in Strasbourg."

"But you will have duties to perform as a married man."

I reflected upon his words for a moment. "Yes, so I have been told. But I honestly do not know if I am capable of that. And what about you? Won't your parents expect you to marry soon?"

"I will not marry another. I am already married."

"But your family, won't they insist?"

"My mother knows about us and will not insist."

I was shocked. "You told her?"

He laughed. "No, she told me."

"What?"

"She is a very perceptive woman. It did not take her long to understand us. Especially after that night you visited us, and we played

94

music."

"And she is not angry? Did she tell your father?"

"No to both of your questions."

Just then, I heard the sound of horses and a carriage pulling up in front of the house. I jumped out of bed, rushed to the window, and saw my family alighting from our carriage; and at the same time, the drovers arrived with our new stallion.

"Dress!" I shouted. "I have not watched the hour closely enough." I rushed to him and took him in my arms as he was trying to put on his pants. He struggled and laughed. But I held tightly, as though it would be our last time together, for I did not know when we would be able to share this bed again.

I must stop here now. I am overcome with the thoughts of what is to come. I need to prepare myself to continue later.

Fifteenth of May 1347

Despite my great heartache, I must complete this narrative.

Not long after that Sunday when Sevaric and I had shared my bed, there came a morning when breakfast was very tense and unusually strange. My father was restless and would not look me in the eye. I suspected that he and my mother had quarreled and dismissed it as a family matter that did not concern me.

I appeared at the warehouse, prepared to work, expecting to find Sevaric, who was usually there before me. I enquired of the other workers if they had seen him; I thought perhaps he had gone on an errand. But he had not been seen at all that day.

I went to the counting room and began my work. I became engrossed in some accounts and was slow to react when the door opened. I looked up with a great smile, expecting to see Sevaric, but instead beheld my father. He had a very grim expression, and I began to suspect that his behavior that morning at breakfast might have concerned me without my knowing it.

"Good morning, again, Father," I tried to greet him with some welcome in my voice. "We have not seen you here for some time. Is there a problem?" I began to suspect that he was going to chastise me for some improper accounts or that there might be a problem with the upcoming shearing.

"You are to come with me now," was all he said, but it was very clear that there was some great trouble at hand.

I arose from my table and accompanied him, not into the warehouse as I expected, but out to the street and toward the town square. He grabbed my arm with great force, hurting me, and led me forward without a single word.

"Father, what is going on? Please explain to me what the trouble is." I was beginning to become deeply frightened.

"I saw you—during your trip to Strasbourg. You and that boy—kissing in a field. Such indecency. I have been troubled about you for some time. Now I know why."

"You? How?"

"The day of your departure for Strasbourg, I needed to present you with some letters that I wanted delivered. You were already gone when I arrived at the warehouse. I followed after and came upon the both of you while you were stopped in that field."

"Then why didn't you present yourself to us?"

"I was not alone. Magistrate Baldoc had accompanied me. We were so shocked I did not know how to proceed. We returned home."

"Oh God." I looked around me, hoping to see Sevaric. "Where is he? What will happen?"

"Your family name has saved you, Lad, but there must be consequences."

"Where are we going? Where is Sevaric? Has something happened to him?"

"You best be concerned only for yourself, just now. It has taken a great effort on my part to keep you out of this."

"Father..."

By now, we had reached the town square. There was quite a large crowd pushing toward the center, and it was growing by the minute. My father pulled me into a doorway and up a flight of stairs at the town hall.

96

We emerged into an empty chamber. He pulled me over to a small balcony, and we stood looking down on the square below. In the center of the square was a scaffold with a central pillar and, surrounding it, a large construction of faggots for a fire. I knew immediately what it was and turned to flee, desperate to find Sevaric and save him. My father, being a much stronger man than I, grabbed me and held me firmly, forcing me to take in the scene as it unfolded below.

My father gave a nod to someone I could not see, and immediately Sevaric appeared in the company of several officers. His mother rushed forward and clung to him, screaming and crying. She was pulled violently away, and Sevaric was led directly to the scaffold and tied securely to the central pillar. His arms were not restricted so that he would be allowed to pray. He was close enough so that I could clearly see his face. He was not in fear. He scanned the crowd, saw me, and smiled his secret smile. I could not cry out to him as my father had his hand over my mouth so I would not betray myself.

The crowd started to become restless and agitated. They pushed in closer to the center. A magistrate read out a proclamation accusing Sevaric of sodomy and unnatural acts against God, and the crowd responded with cries of, "Light the faggots! Light the faggots! Burn!"

The magistrate raised his hand, and the crowd quieted momentarily. He gestured toward two men standing by the side with lighted torches. They came forward and touched the fire to the base of the prepared woodpile. The flames shot quickly upwards. The crowd became frantic, chanting their cries of, "Burn," and dancing wildly around the pyre as though it was a special holiday.

Sevaric remained calm. He spoke not a word, but having found me, his gaze never left me. He reached up with his free hand and pulled out the ring on the chain around his neck. He held it out toward me until the flames engulfed him, and his head fell forward, like when I had seen him nod off, just before he fell asleep at my side. I closed my eyes, still securely in my father's arms, but no tears would come. For me there was only the smell of his burning flesh.

☆☆☆

Twentieth of May 1347

Our worst fears are being realized. I have heard reports that a case of the plague has been discovered in the village. I have been conferring with my family about what course of action we must all take, but there have been no firm plans yet formed. I feel even more urgency now to complete my tale.

After Sevaric's death, I refused to set foot ever again in the warehouse. I confined myself to my chambers for weeks. I refused to take meals with the family, and I would not speak with my father. Twice I tried escaping, hoping to head for Paris, but each time my father and his men caught up with me and forced me home, driving me deeper into my seclusion.

My father decided he needed to move the wedding up to September, incorrectly believing that the love of a true woman would be my cure. Never was there a more recalcitrant groom. I have to admit that I was most cruel to my poor bride. She does not deserve me, and I pray that one day she might find herself a true lover. For my part, I shall never seek, nor do I expect to find, the quality of love that I so richly experienced with Sevaric. I have been told that in time wounds heal, pain fades, and yes, even love will diminish. I have, as of yet, not found that to be true.

It has been just over half a year now since I lost all that I was, or ever hoped to be. I exist—yes, just exist. Each day I awake, move through my duties of the day, and retire once again—alone in my own bed. I have not returned to the pond, nor ever expect to. I abide with that sweet woman whom I honor as my wife, but do not love. And our childlessness galls my father; and I feel that it is just retribution for his hateful actions toward me.

I am now up to date with my story. I do not know if this is the end of my narration or not. I know there is no end to my sorrow. These few lines have given me comfort as I wander back in my mind to the time in my life when I was truly alive. I do not see how I can endure the remainder of my time here on earth, and long solely to be reunited with my Sevaric in our special place. Only time and God's will can reveal when that will be.

I will put these pages aside for now, and later, if there is anything of importance to report, I shall return. If not, then I turn this poor narrative over to my destiny and remain...

Warin of the House of Thann

☆☆☆

Twenty-second of August 1347

I awoke this morning with a pain so deep that I can hardly breathe. It is one year ago today that Sevaric was taken from me. But I must not dwell on that now. There is no time to waste. The plague has ravaged our area. With great sorrow, I must report the death of my two sisters, my mother, and my wife. My father is not well and will probably not survive.

While I am still well, I feel that I must flee this area. I have requested, and been invited, to reside with the brothers at the Ascenseur monastery. It is my understanding that all there are still well, and they have carefully sealed themselves off from the surrounding pestilence. They are self-sufficient and require no outside assistance to continue in their good health. I am very grateful that they will allow me to join them.

It is time now for me to depart. I shall report more later if there are any further developments of consequence.

☆☆☆

Ninth of September 1347

How much anguish can a single person endure? All around me is falling into ruin. My father did, indeed, perish. The infection has entered the monastery and many of the brothers have fallen victim to the plague. For some reason, I have been spared. I do all that I can each day to tend to those who are ill, but there is no treatment, and I fall into bed each night exhausted from my duties. And it is a great effort now to write even these few brief words. I can write no more this evening.

☆☆☆

Third of October 1347

There is little time left now. I too have become a victim of this disease. I am covered in blisters and can barely drink even a small amount of water, though I have a high fever, and at times find myself falling into delirium.

I feel my life has prepared me well for my end, and I look forward with such great joy to my final release. Oh, my beloved, Sevaric, I shall soon be with you.

☆☆☆

(The following is written in a hand other than that of the author of this manuscript)

Tenth of October 1347

Sevaric, I am with you now.

Fly Boys

Wearing its coat of ice
The shriveled apple enfolds the sleeping seed,
Dreaming of moist warm earth.

Haruki repeatedly struck at the ice on the pond with a large bone. The geese waddled down to the bank's edge from their shelter, grateful for the opportunity to drink, swim, and preen in open water, dressed by the falling snow. Haruki gazed out across the ice-locked pond to the charcoal-stenciled trees on the opposite bank. He watched a solitary child in a red parka mournfully kicking a yellow ball in circles—no companion to play with. Haruki shook the last of the cracked corn from the paper bag, and a few of the geese glided out of the pond to peck at the latest offering.

Walking back to the house, Haruki felt the cold in his arthritic joints. He leaned heavily on his cane. He paused halfway back, even though it was but a short distance. He could see his wife, Kazuko, kneeling at the altar arranging a few branches of spring peach blossoms, imported from the south, an echo of what was soon to come. He envied that she could kneel like that, as it was such a great effort for him to kneel or raise himself from the floor when he rolled out his sleeping mat before bedtime.

At eighty-five years old, he had few joys left but memories. Not that he was angry or bitter. He had had a good life. But he and his wife had no children, and that had left her, if not bitter, then at least sad and disappointed. Fortunately, she had some grandnieces and nephews who continued to care for her; and living close by, they would visit frequently with gifts, attention, and invitations to family festivals.

Haruki slid back the door and came into the house. He removed his scarf and was about to hang it on a peg on the wall.

"Could you please bring in some more charcoal before you take off your coat?—if it's not a great inconvenience to you," Kazuko asked in the baby-doll voice that infuriated Haruki with its subservience. She rose from the altar, went over to the fire pit in the center of the room and poked at the coals under the lightly simmering teakettle suspended by a hook over the fire. "I'll have some nice hot tea for you when you come back in," she added.

Without answering, Haruki once more put on his scarf, went outside to the charcoal bin at the end of the porch, and filled up the bucket with the bamboo scoop.

Haruki and Arashi both reached for the bamboo cup at the same time. It floated on top of the basin of cool water used for drinking—just outside the Air Force barracks. Their hands touched, and an electric shock raced up Haruki's arm. He looked up, confused and cautious. He was greeted with a sly smile from another young pilot, a good few inches taller than he was and slender. His face was etched like a fine Samurai sword—lean and chiseled—like tempered steel. But his eyes smiled softly and playfully like the sun dancing on the surface of the drinking water. Haruki felt blossoms gently opening in the pit of his stomach.

Haruki lugged the full bucket of charcoal back into the house and over to the fire pit. Kazuko smiled, nodded three times sharply, uttered a breathy "thank you," and began placing pieces of charcoal on the coals with tongs.

Haruki went back over to the pegs in the wall, took off his scarf again, and hung his coat next to the peg with the solitary white silk scarf. Haruki's eyes lingered on the scarf for a long moment, and when he looked over to his wife, she quickly glanced away, embarrassed to be seen staring at her husband, knowing what that scarf meant to him.

"Your tea is ready now," she almost whispered.

Haruki took the cup from her without a word and shuffled to his room, sliding the door softly behind him, settling in at his desk, and staring out the window at the still falling, early spring snow on this very gray afternoon. A single flash of sunlight suddenly shot through the clouds and blazed upon the red figure playing across the pond.

Looking up, the swallow's wing
Slashes across the face of the sun.
What a sweet blink!

Haruki rested on his hoe and watched the robins weaving their nest at the top of the apricot tree now in full bloom. He always enjoyed preparing the garden for planting. It was still too early to put out the tomato or eggplant starts, but he felt good preparing the ground for an early May planting. Kazuko opened a packet of mizuna seeds, a cold-resistant green she could plant early in the season. She created a furrow in the row and began tapping the seeds into the soil before covering them up with loose soil and watering.

Having finished the last row, Haruki put the hoe away in the shed and took out the rake. He glanced out over the pond as a flight of wild ducks skimmed over the surface before landing by the rushes at the far end. The sun caught the iridescent feathers of a male mallard as he landed, creating a dance of color in the cattails. Haruki began raking the last of the leaves under the wisteria that hung over the porch, just now putting out its first tender leaves.

Kazuko took off her work gloves and placed them on the bench by the door before going inside to prepare lunch. They retained the form of her hands as they lay there, looking like they were about to strangle the bottle of fish emulsion fertilizer.

"Here, I think you dropped this," Arashi said, tapping Haruki on the shoulder. Haruki turned around and accepted the glove that Arashi had picked up.

For a reason he couldn't understand, Haruki blushed and could only stammer out a faint "Thank you." He paused before asking, "Have you been following me?"

"Maybe." Arashi grinned broadly and put his hand on Haruki's shoulder. "Sake?" he offered, pointing down a narrow side street. Haruki nodded.

"A man of few words, I like that. I, myself, talk far too much. You will get to know that about me." Arashi laughed, taking Haruki by the arm and leading him down the street to an almost hidden bar, chatting about the upcoming air drills.

Haruki wondered why Arashi would take him to such a shabby, out of the way establishment. It was dark inside, and there was not even a sign outside announcing that this was a sake bar. But as his eyes adjusted to the darkness, he could see that the clientele were all young men. Haruki stopped short with a slight twinge of panic and a resurgence of old, hidden fears. He turned to leave but Arashi entreated softly, "Please don't go."

"But..." Haruki couldn't quite find the words.

"It's all right. Never been to a place like this before?"

"I think perhaps you misunderstand..." Haruki tried to explain.

"I don't think so," Arashi whispered in Haruki's ear. *"It's just unfamiliar. But if you let me lead you, I'm sure I can make you feel very much at home."*

Haruki watched a boisterous, silly game show on the television as Kazuko squinted by the light of her lamp, patching the edges of a worn comforter. Haruki turned off the television with the remote in his lap and sat in silence for a moment. The wind outside was picking up, knocking a branch against Kazuko's bedroom window.

"I promise I'll get to that branch tomorrow," Haruki offered. "I keep forgetting about it except when it's windy."

Neither spoke for a moment. Then Kazuko put her sewing things aside in a lacquer box and turned off the light. She folded the comforter and headed toward the bedrooms. "I'll put this in your room. Sleep well." She disappeared down the hallway toward his bedroom. She left the comforter for him and quietly retreated to her own room and slid shut the door. The house was now in darkness except for a faint light coming from the open door of Haruki's room and the light of the half-moon spilling through the windows overlooking the pond. Haruki continued to sit in his chair, lost in the silence of the house. The wind moaned and whistled gently through the windows. The faint glow of charcoal embers pulsed in the fire pit. Part of the fire collapsed, and the coals flared up into a single flame for just a brief moment and then subsided back into the last glow of the dying fire.

☆☆☆

The tardy summer shower
Dances on the parched earth.
Tickling the gasping grasses.

The horses danced out from the Takizawa Soozen Jinja shrine. *Changu changu* rang the horse's bells. One hundred costumed horse dancers began their parade to the Hachimangu shrine fifteen kilometers away. The Changu-Changu Umakko festival was just getting underway on this hot June Saturday—a celebration of the end of the planting season and a prayer for a bountiful harvest to come.

"They look like they're going to be very hot today. I hope they have enough water," Kazuko commented to her grandnephew, Juro, about the horse dancers. She searched in her carrier for her water bottle and Haruki's cap and offered them to him. "Don't get dehydrated." She shook the bottle at him. He took it without comment and took a deep swig. He refused the cap, however, waving it away.

Juro offered to buy them some ices and ambled over toward the ice stall, having seen a very pretty young girl heading that way.

Haruki turned away slightly from Kazuko and tucked the white silk scarf tighter inside his kimono so Kazuko would not see that he was wearing it today. Juro returned with three ices and the pretty young girl. He handed a mandarin orange ice to Kazuko, a watermelon ice to Haruki, and shared a honeydew melon and lime ice with Choko, the young girl who giggled when they both licked the ice at the same time.

Kazuko was enchanted with the dancing horses and threw the paper flowers that she had been making for weeks at them to show her appreciation. She bobbed in excitement as the parade of floats with ecstatic drummers thundered by.

Haruki glimpsed a tall, thin young man on the other side of the street. His handsome, chiseled face flashed a smile and then he disappeared into the crowd. Haruki licked at the watermelon ice.

105

Haruki leaned back against Arashi's naked chest. They were seated on the porch of Arashi's family hunting lodge, high in the mountains. A waterfall and stream tumbled not more than twenty meters away. Both were naked and trying to cool themselves in this August heat by eating slices of iced watermelon that dribbled juice down their chests. They were playing a little game to see who could spit the watermelon seeds the farthest.

"Ah! The record so far," Arashi crowed, having ejected a seed a good three meters. The world record—or so he said. Haruki didn't respond to the taunt and was very quiet. Arashi looked down at him. "You all right?" he asked, tilting Haruki's head up so he could see his eyes.

"Oh yes," Haruki replied looking up into Arashi's face. "I just didn't know."

"What didn't you know?"

"That I could be this happy."

Arashi bent forward and leaned his chin on the top of Haruki's head. "Yeah, I figured that." He laughed and then thought for a moment and added, "Then why do you seem so sad?"

"Because I don't know what happens next."

"How do you mean?"

"I don't know how to live this way. What do we do now? It's very nice here—up in the mountains, far away, no people, just us—but what do we do when we get back? How can we be together—out there?" Haruki's gesture embraced the whole world.

Arashi didn't speak for a moment. He just nodded, thinking. "Yeah, I know. Not easy."

"There's no way for us to be alone at the barracks. And our families—I am to be married to a very sweet girl in the autumn. What about that?" Haruki was becoming agitated, and he turned around to face Arashi. "And what about you and your family? Don't they want you to marry?"

"I'm not the eldest. And I have a lot of brothers and sisters. I could slip through the cracks without a lot of trouble."

"But I'm an only child. You know what that means."

106

"I do."

"And the war? What if we get separated? I don't know if I could bear that."

Haruki became even more agitated, and he threw his arms around Arashi and pulled him closely to him and started kissing him passionately. However, both being naked they soon became aroused and ended up making love on the porch covered in watermelon juice and other substances. When they were done, they raced to the stream and threw themselves in the water like a couple of truant kids escaping school.

Juro closed the car doors after Kazuko and Haruki climbed out of their seats with a little effort. Juro supported Kazuko's arm and led her back to the house. He was a good kid—thoughtful and considerate. She patted his hand when he delivered her to the front door.

"Thank you, my dear. It's been a lovely outing."

Choko was still in the front seat of the car, waiting for Juro to return so they could get back to his apartment for a little quality time alone.

Juro gave Kazuko a quick kiss on the top of her head and scurried back to his car without waving good-bye.

"Are you hungry?" Kazuko asked Haruki, who was standing at the windows looking out over the pond.

"Not yet," he answered and slid open the door and walked out to inspect the garden, now in its full fruiting. He carried a basket and a pair of shears, and gathered a few cucumbers, a handful of slender eggplants, and a dark purple and a yellow heirloom tomato. He put the basket on the porch and wandered down to the edge of the pond as the sun was just setting behind the trees on the far shore. The nail clipping of a new moon hung like a delicate smile just above the fading horizon.

Haruki pulled at the silk scarf still hidden by the folds of his kimono. He took it out, felt the silk against his cheek, and then tied it around his neck as the landscape before him began to sink into darkness.

☆☆☆

The last golden leaf
Desperately clutches the mother branch.

But is no match for the icy wind.

The first frost had taken out the tomatoes, the basil, and a few of the other less hardy garden plants. It always saddened Haruki to have to cut back the dead stalks. There was still some kale, Brussels sprouts, and cabbage that actually thrived in the colder weather. He cast a plastic sheet over a few of the other more tender plants that had been spared the first frost. It was going to be another freezing night tonight and he wanted to save as many plants as he could.

Kazuko had slipped getting out of the bathtub last week and was still in the hospital with a broken hip. He would be going there later, after lunch, to read to her for an hour or so. And it was becoming increasingly difficult for him to get around without his cane, even for a short period of time. He could not get out of any chair now without its assistance.

He put together a bouquet from the bed of chrysanthemums under the red maple tree by the front gate to take to Kazuko. He put them in a bucket of water by the back door, intending to tie them together with a nice ribbon from her sewing box just before he left for the hospital. Kazuko's grandniece, Emiko, was going to pick him up at two.

Haruki was not that hungry, but he sliced open a persimmon and squeezed a little lime juice on it. He went to his bedroom and sat at his desk to sort the mail and pay a few bills. He opened his desk drawer to take out the checkbook. Underneath was the letter—the only one he had ever received from Arashi. It had been a very long time since he last looked at it. He took it out of the envelope, opened it, and read.

Haruki, I know how you hate me for what I am about to do. But I have to do this for my country. Please forgive me. Know that I will be thinking of you when I strike. I will love you always. Arashi

Haruki bowed his head and let the letter fall onto his lap. He stared across the room to the small table with the faded photograph of Arashi hanging on the wall above. He pulled himself out of his chair, the letter falling to the floor, and hobbled over to the table. He took some incense out of the table drawer and lit it. The smoke rose up around his head and languidly curled over toward the photo, wafting like a curtain, caressed by a surprisingly warm autumn afternoon breeze.

"How can you ever make me understand?" Haruki asked, tears streaming down his face. Smoke from a thousand sticks of incense filled the temple. Arashi turned from him and walked toward the entrance, his back to the golden reclining Buddha. Haruki raced after him and caught him by the shoulder, turning him sharply around, and taking Arashi's white silk scarf in both of his hands—fighting a strong temptation to strangle him with it.

Arashi slapped Haruki in the face. "Get a hold on yourself. You're making a scene. Is this how you want to remember our last day together?"

Haruki was so startled he let go of the scarf. Arashi turned and walked down the temple steps to the street. Haruki raced after. Arashi wouldn't speak to him again till they were back in the hotel room, and then he turned to Haruki, took off his scarf, put it around Haruki's neck and took him tightly in his arms, unable to speak and unable to let him go.

Haruki carefully picked up the letter from the floor and inserted it back into its envelope. He put it back in the drawer and closed it. He sat back in the desk chair and stared out across the pond. An apple fell from a tree down by the pond, rolled down the bank, and splashed into the still water by the dock. A goose swimming nearby scurried over, snapped it up, and downed it with one quick swallow.

It was a quarter till two. Haruki got out of his chair, went to Kazuko's sewing box, took out a ribbon and went to the back door. He wrapped the ribbon around the chrysanthemums and went back inside to get his coat and hat. He locked up the house and stood by the front gate waiting for Kazuko's grandniece to pick him up and take him to the hospital. The leaves from the red maple fell in his hair and across the shoulders of his black coat.

The incense under Arashi's photograph burned out and sighed up the last little breath of smoke before going cold. Across the pond, a bullfrog leaped off a lily pad to grab a low-flying dragonfly, splashing gleefully into the water and sending a spray into the air. The splash was caught by the sun, which shot a ray of light across the pond into Haruki's room, lighting up Arashi's Kamikaze headband with the rising sun in the middle of his forehead.

Madam Macadam

Seth's ma, Sally, was wondering what to do about her son's sexual education. Here she had a sprightly boy, just eighteen, and already the man of the house—her husband lost at Vicksburg years ago. Her great-aunt had left Sally a parcel of land and a cabin in Colorado not far from the mining towns. With no husband, one boy child, and no other prospects, she had headed west from Kentucky where they had been staying with her parents during the war. Her daddy had resisted her leaving, but she was resolute, and catching a train to Missouri, they headed west along the Santa Fe Trail till they branched off toward Henderson with their newly purchased wagon, supplies, a cow, and a mule. Seth was only six years old at the time and not worth nothin' when it came to working the land. But her great-aunt had also left Sally a small inheritance, which she used to hire a hand for plowing, and they had eked out a living till Seth grew and was able to contribute more to running the farm. By then they had sheep, cattle, and chickens as well as crops, and Seth grew big and strong and handsome and was such a blessing to his Ma.

Sally knew it was a "man's" job to educate a son in matters of the heart, but she had no one to turn to. She couldn't ask the Reverend Kincaid. He would "tut-tut" and pretend he didn't hear her. No, she needed another source. The only one she felt safe turning to about this was Mr. Calder, the grocer.

She made a special effort to look nice when she went into his grocery store for her weekly shopping. She had sent Seth off to the livery stable to see if the harness they had ordered had come in yet. She obviously couldn't have Seth around when she made her enquiry of Mr. Calder.

"Now then, will that be all, Mrs. Sherwin?" Calder asked, as he put the last items in Sally's basket.

111

Sally hesitated, but finally leaned in and whispered, "Might I have a private word with you, Mr. Calder?"

"If it's about your bill, you needn't worry. Your credit is always good with me."

"No sir," she answered, "it's about another, more personal matter concerning my son."

"I see. Of course, how can I help you?" he asked, scooting along the counter toward the back of the store where they could speak more privately.

"Well, this is really embarrassing, but you see Seth is eighteen now...and he's...well, you know, almost a grown man. And as there's no man in the house. I feel it's time for him to know a few things...You understand?" She hoped Mr. Calder would get her inference.

"I see," he said, stroking his chin and feeling very nervous. "You need someone to discuss the facts of life with the lad. Is that what you're saying?"

"Yes, sir. That's it exactly. And I was wondering if you might..." Mr. Calder looked startled. "Well you, or somebody you could refer me to. The Reverend Kincaid would be more than useless."

Mr. Calder laughed. "Well, you certainly are right on that point, Mrs. Sherwin. Poor old dear would turn twenty shades of purple and red and have an attack of apoplexy. Sure as we both are standin' right here." They laughed.

Sally looked up pleadingly to the grocer. "Can you suggest anyone? I would be ever so grateful."

Calder pondered for a moment and then suggested, "Well, there is one person I could think of, but it's not a man. In fact, it's someone who could both instruct your son and also provide him with a very necessary service."

Sally was puzzled. "What kind of service?"

"Well, let's just say she could provide a comprehensive introduction to the mysteries of love and romance," Calder hedged.

Sally was shocked. "You mean...?"

Calder nodded. "I do."

"Oh, well. I don't know...That seems a bit unorthodox. I'm not sure we should go that far."

"Well, you think about it. If you decide you would like to proceed, just let me know, and I will make the arrangements."

"What is this person's name, might I ask?"

"Madam Macadam—she runs an establishment over on the west edge of town. It is popularly frequented by some of the most upstanding members of our community and the very best of your traveling gentry."

"I see. Well, thank you, I shall consider your suggestion and get back to you. My, I never expected such a solution to my predicament."

Seth already knew all about reproduction. Hell, he'd been raising and breeding farm animals since he was ten. Now his ma was getting all up in his face about something she wanted him to do, but she would never really come out and honestly talk about it. He had a suspicion that she wanted to introduce him to some female or other. But she was just too embarrassed to proceed.

Seth was tall and strong. He kept his blond hair cut short and wore a straw hat he'd picked up in the feed store. He didn't much mind how he dressed, as he always had a ton of chores and had to dress ready to work at all times. Only time he changed into his one nice shirt and put on a coat was for church at his mother's insistence.

He couldn't remember when he first started waking up in the morning with what he called his stiffy. It didn't take him long, though, to figure out how to work on that. Oh man, he sure enjoyed rubbin' one out. At first it was purely physical—just a way of releasing the tension. But then he began to visualize himself touching the Carter boy's chest, or he'd find himself getting a stiffy when he was at the stables in town buying grain, and he'd see Cal Tolliver leaning over to pick up sacks to load onto the wagon. Heavens, that kid had a nice behind. When he did that in those tight pants of his, it drove poor Seth to distraction. One time Cal turned around quickly with two sacks in his arms for loading on the wagon. Cal caught Seth staring at him intently and smiled. Seth blushed and quickly shook out the mule's reins, and headed toward home before the wagon was even fully loaded. That night when he worked his stiffy all Seth could see was Cal's tight pants, and all he could think about was what it would be like to kiss that handsome smiling face—and those inviting lips.

That can't be right, Seth pondered as he pitched feed to the cattle. He never saw two male animals goin' at it. Well, except for the two rams. Oh yeah, he'd forgotten about them. He finally had to keep the rams separated. But he also knew all the young fellas in town were always moonin' over some filly. And the girls were sighin' and flutterin' their eyes over some buck. Sure didn't do nothin' for him, though. That Callie Jameson was always comin' over to him in the grocer's and pullin' at his sleeve and leanin' up against him when he was tryin' to concentrate on his mother's shoppin' list. She'd flutter her hands and all but bark in her efforts to get his attention. He couldn't get outta there fast enough when she was around.

☆☆☆

Sally had thought long and hard about Mr. Calder's suggestion. It went against all her church-goin' upbringin' to agree, but ultimately she felt she had no choice. Mr. Calder set a date for Sally to take Seth to Madam Macadam's establishment on a Thursday night. That night was chosen as it would be less busy than the weekend, and Seth could be given more exacting, personal attention.

Seth sat working on his math figures at the table by the kerosene lamp. His ma gave him most of his learnin', as he was needed on the farm, and couldn't take time off to go into town for ordinary schoolin'. Seth looked up and saw his ma standing before him, silent, and with her hands nervously working her handkerchief. This, he knew, meant she had concerns. "Ma? You want sumpin'?"

"Oh yes, Seth." She hurriedly pulled up a chair and sat opposite him at the table.

"Oka-a-y...what?"

"We're gonna be goin' into town Thursday night."

"Some church thing?"

"No dear, it's sumpin' for you."

"What kind of *sumpin'*?"

114

Sally was working the handkerchief real hard now. "You ain't got no pa, and it just seems time for you to get some instruction on matters that a ma just can't broach to a son." She leaned forward. "You understand?"

He did. Then he thought through the implications of this. It was pretty clear in his own mind that he was like the two rams, but he also knew that there seemed to be no place for him in this world if he was like that. He concluded it might be all right if someone knowledgeable about these matters could advise him. He sure couldn't talk about these things to his ma.

"Where we goin' then?"

"A place called Madam Macadam's. You ever hear of it?" Seth nodded. "You ever been there?"

"No, ma'am."

"I could take you there, but I'm guessin' you'd rather go there by yourself. They'll be expectin' ya. And all's paid for. So no need to worry yourself about that."

Seth nodded again. "Well...I guess there's a first time for everything."

☆☆☆

Josephina Macadam had been a stunning beauty in her day. Not that she wasn't still a looker, but she was a bit shopworn, some ungracious souls might say. But she had once reigned at the very top of her profession during her glory days in St. Louis, Chicago, and Denver.

Her last establishment in Denver had been destroyed in a fire, and a number of her girls had perished. She had no alternative but to flee, as the circumstances of the fire were whispered about as being suspect. There were suggestions that perhaps financial strain might have prompted the fire for insurance purposes.

So Josephina found new quarters in Henderson and set up a fine shop. She was doing a nice, brisk business with her stable of comely young ladies, especially with the neighboring hills yielding fair amounts of gold for ready spending.

Now Josephina was not your ordinary blowsy madam—too old to attract customers and made up like a circus clown with far too much makeup—a caricature of an appealing woman. No, she was stately. She was tall, thin, and dressed simply, but with great taste. Her silver hair was piled high on her head and fastened with what looked like a jewel-encrusted coronet.

Her establishment from the outside looked like any ordinary middle-class dwelling. There was no sign announcing services. There was no red light. There were no dark, heavy, red velvet drapes with gold swags. The rooms were light and airy. Of course the girl's rooms were curtained for privacy. And Madam's special signature were her birds— parrots, cockatoos, finches, canaries, mynah birds—all singing, squawking, and shouting out words fit only for a gang of pirates.

Seth entered the house, removing his hat like a polite lad. Madam spotted him immediately and went over.

"You must be Seth." She smiled and extended her hand.

"Yes, ma'am." He was not nervous, but he *was* cautious and circumspect.

Madam led him into the living room where there was a large collection of comfortably stuffed sofas and chairs. As it was still early in the evening, before the hour when most of the clientele arrived, there was a large assortment of wares on display. Seth looked around and smiled and nodded politely to the girls.

"Seth, why don't you come with me to my office? Before we get down to business I should like to get to know you better and get a sense of how we might best serve you as you are a new customer."

She led the way to a large, comfortable office where most of her menagerie of birds were prancing and preening in their cages.

"Please sit," she indicated, as she settled behind her impressive desk. "Now then, I understand you are a virgin and need some instruction in the ways of romance. Is that correct?"

"Well, ma'am, it is indeed true that I ain't never had no lovin' before, but I'm not without some knowledge. I do raise a parcel of animals after all."

Madam laughed. "Yes, I see. That certainly would provide ample instruction in the ways of—if not romance, then at least the basics in fornication." She studied him admiringly. "You are one very fine lookin' young man. Can't imagine you would have any trouble attracting the young ladies. Am I not right?"

"Well, ma'am, that would seem to be the case."

"So we don't need to provide you with a mercy fuck, I would imagine."

Seth laughed. "No, ma'am, whatever that means."

"Well, we get a lot of young men in here who are...how shall I put this delicately...fuckin' ugly. They are brought in because they couldn't get laid if they was the last standing stud on the planet. But that's not your problem, is it?"

"I surely hope not."

"So how come you need our services? I would think there would be a line a young ladies stretchin' down the block just hankerin' to ride that sweet cock of yours."

Seth blushed at her language.

"Well, ma'am, let's just say I live a ways out of town, and I live with my ma. Not much opportunity for romance. And to be honest, haven't exactly had my head turned by any of the young ladies in this town yet."

"Really? Interesting. Well, if you think you might be ready, let's go back and see if any of *my* young ladies can turn your head."

They went back into living room where the girls were waiting and posing with the hopes of being chosen. They didn't often get the chance to entertain a real looker—most of their clients hadn't even *washed* in a month.

"So what appeals to you? Redhead, brunette, blonde, thin, hefty, big titties, small titties, big ass, kinky, vanilla? What's your flavor?"

Seth looked around the room—no one really striking his fancy. He just lifted his hand and pointed to the one in front of him. "That one's okay."

"Cherie? Surprising choice, but it's not for me to say."

Cherie was at the upper end of the age range. Her blonde hair was obviously out of a bottle, and she had neglected her roots a little too long. And as to her proportions—in polite company she would be referred to as having an 'ample' figure. She seemed as surprised as the madam that he had selected her. But she was ready, willing, and able.

Her room was stark and functional. There was no attempt to create a romantic atmosphere. Her customers were not there for romance. Her one concession to mood was to turn down the oil lamp. She took off her negligee and her tits, finally released from the garment, plopped down like two pigeons landing on a porch. She turned to Seth.

"Need help, honey?" she asked, as he was making no effort to get undressed.

She went over and began to unbutton his shirt.

"That's all right, I can do that." He removed his shirt.

Cherie reached down and unbuttoned his pants fly. She put her hand inside and grabbed his cock. "Oh honey, I see we got some work to do here. You're limp as an old rope." She laughed. "Come on over." She led the way to the bed.

Seth had removed his pants and underwear. He was naked and shivering. The room was not as warm as he'd expected. Or was he shivering for some other reason? Cherie patted the edge of the bed.

"Better come over here and let me see what I can do to get your candy ready."

Seth sat on the edge of the bed, and Cherie kneeled down between his legs and began working him with her mouth. Absolutely nothing was happening. Cherie's jaw was getting tired and she stopped and looked up at Seth.

"Not workin', is it, hon?"

"Seems not," he replied.

Cherie got up off the floor, put her negligee on again, and stood looking at Seth. "I got an idea. Be right back." She left the room and was gone for what seemed to be a very long time. Seth was getting cold and wrapped the top bed sheet around his shoulders.

Finally, there was a knock at the door. Seth was surprised Cherie needed to knock at her own door. "Yeah," Seth called out.

The door opened, and in the dim light, Seth strained to see who it was. Then the figure said softly, "Madam thinks I might be able to help you." The figure walked in, shutting the door behind. Stepping forward into the circle of light from the lamp, and unbuttoning his shirt, Cal Tolliver came toward Seth.

Seth was completely dumbfounded.

"Got myself a part-time job here at the house. Sometimes we get clients with special needs," Cal spoke softly as he finished undressing. "Madam prides herself in running a full service establishment. We mean to please *everyone*."

Cal came up to Seth, who was still sitting on the edge of the bed. He straddled Seth from behind, wrapped his arms around Seth and slowly removed the sheet from around Seth's shoulders. Cal buried his lips in the crook of Seth's neck and began kissing him, working his way up to Seth's ear, sending shivers through his whole being. It was *very* clear that Seth would no longer have any problem getting *his* candy "ready" now. In fact, there was nothing at all hesitant in Seth's reaction. He turned to Cal, looked into his eyes, and said, "You have no idea how much I've wanted this."

"Oh yes, I do," Cal replied. "I've seen you watching me. Undressing me with your eyes and eating me up alive."

They both laughed and fell upon the bed in a tangle of limbs and sheets.

☆☆☆

It was just getting light when Seth awoke, his arm around Cal's chest. Cal's deep, steady breathing was a miracle to Seth. He brushed his lips against the back of Cal's head. He sighed deeply. He pulled the sheet up to cover them both from the chill morning air. Cal stirred and turned toward Seth, grabbing him up in his arms. "Good morning, you beautiful man, you," he said in his husky, early morning voice. Tears trickled down Seth's cheeks. Cal reached up and wiped them away. "Hey, hey, you okay, baby?"

Seth managed to say, "I had no idea."

"I know. First time getting what you really want is pretty awesome, huh? Kinda like a religious experience, isn't it?" Cal ruffled Seth's hair and planted a really soft and tender kiss on his lips.

"But what now?" Seth asked, still confused and adjusting to his new reality.

"What do you mean? It's all paid for."

Seth was jolted. "That's not what I meant. Is that all I am to you? An assignment—a job?"

Cal smiled. "Is that what you believe?"

"I don't know. It sure seemed more than that to me last night."

"Yeah, me too," Cal said, caressing Seth's cheek.

"Then where do we go from here? I ain't never gonna go with no women. Never gonna get married."

"Now, now, now. Not so fast. Don't go gettin' ahead a yourself."

Seth sat up. He really wanted to talk this through. His life had changed, and he needed to get clear on what this meant for him. "Are there a lot of men like us?"

"Some. Not a lot out here, but enough. You see a lot more in the cities."

"What are we called?"

"Sodomites, twilight people, and some other not too nice names."

Seth was thoughtful. "And what about us—you and me?"

Cal was hesitant and looked away. "I'm getting married in six months, ya know."

Seth was jolted. "No. No."

"Imagine you will too, one day. How else you gonna keep the farm, raise kids to carry on? You know how it is. You got no brothers or sisters. It's all on you, Seth."

"So you just gonna get married and knife out that part a yourself?"

"Hell no. There's always ways to meet guys. Get a bit of fun. Carry on."

"Not me. Sorry, not me." Seth stood up and began getting dressed. "I'm gonna have me a man to love. To be with. To make a life with. Damn the town. Damn my ma. And damn you too, if you gonna be such a coward."

"Oh Seth..." Cal reached out toward Seth as he was about to leave the room. Seth looked back, just once, with a look that pierced Cal to his deepest soul, and which he would never forget as long as he lived.

Cheap Trick in the Drunk Tank

Gordon Kootsmovi was known on the street as Cheap Trick. He hustled for Buds and a few bucks by giving blowjobs in the alleys of Winslow, because he needed the cash—and because he liked it. At eighteen he had escaped from the Hopi First Mesa and hitched down to Winslow to dream his other life. His mother was Spider Woman and his dad was Jack Rabbit. Gordon was a two spirit and needed to play with men that were of his other tribe.

Winslow, Arizona's, population was a squeak under ten thousand. It had a divided main street that ran through town along the railroad with the banks and upright stores a discreet distance from the unsightly tracks. The bars were generally on the side streets at the edges of town where Gordon roamed and where the Harvey Girls still danced and sang in the shadows.

Gordon had been rounded up by the police at three in the morning and deposited in the city clink till daylight—when most of the drunks would have dried out enough to be released once again to forage for stale sandwiches and short flasks of cheap hooch. Gordon was now so well known by law enforcement they didn't even bother to book him anymore. He didn't complain. It gave him a place to spend the rest of the night and catch a few winks before he was booted out way too early after the change of police shifts.

Gordon lay on the hard platform that resembled a bunk in such a way that he could peer out of the single-barred window. He focused on his star. His mother gave it to him in a dream, and it had guided him since he was six. As long as he could see its bright twinkle, he was at peace, whatever the current situation. Now if only he could fall asleep. He gazed up at his star, and as there were fewer than the usual number of winos snoring this early morning, he soon drifted off and stepped into one of his recurring dreams.

The low morning sun had not yet burned off the mists still nestled in the hollows of the sloping lawn. The light shooting through the surrounding trees sent trestles of shadow down toward the languid river. Whispering reeds shuddered in the eddies by the low banks flecked with tiny pink daisies. Ophelia floated in the currents further out, flinging garlands and nosegays at the boatmen in their skiffs wearing their brightly striped rugby jerseys. A giraffe swayed gently toward a rank of dark trees to grab at branches of leaves with its grasping lips. A clown juggled for a group of children in white dresses and scarlet tunics spread out under a massive oak, shading a large portion of the lawn. The bells on Cheap Trick's ankles shook and sparked music everywhere he danced. A spiral of hummingbirds danced a crown above his head. The heavy dark Kachina mask weighed on Cheap Trick's shoulders, which slowed his movements, but he danced on, the rattles in his hands signing out the rhythms of his native chants. Slowly he started to rise above the scene. He could look down now at the entire landscape. The manor house sat atop the estate. The river flowed toward the sea. The clouds swept him along like the river below. Soon he was at sea. His mask was now a boat with sails like painted fortresses with the enemy raising fires below.

But the images were becoming scrambled, and turning his head on the bunk, he was awake.

Only one drunk still drooled in a corner of the cell. Gordon righted himself on the bunk. His star was long gone, and the lemony sun fell on his right knee.

"Okay, Geronimo, time to scoot." Randall ran his billy club along the bars of the cell. Randall was one of the older cops and tended to give Gordon an easier time than some of the younger hardnoses. "Try to stay out of trouble today, okay? I'd really like *not* to see you back in here tomorrow. Can you do that?"

Gordon didn't reply, but picked up his backpack at the front desk and turned back to the cop before he exited and smiled. "See ya soon. Got a corporate board meeting at noon, don't ya know?"

The sergeant laughed. "I'm on graveyard again tonight, so don't let me see you in here *too* early, okay, kid?"

Gordon headed down the street toward the railway hotel. Winslow had been a major stop in the old days for the trains headed to Los Angeles from the east, with another stop just ahead for the Grand Canyon. One of the Harvey chain hotels, it had fallen into disrepair, but was now being spruced up and was beginning to recapture some of its faded glory and cachet. Gordon knew he could find breakfast there in the dumpster and headed to the side of the hotel where he could feast in the shadows, unnoticed till after the breakfast service ended, and the kitchen crew came out for a smoke.

Gordon usually spent his mornings panhandling out at the gas stations on I-40, the east-west highway that bisects Arizona and is a major route to the Grand Canyon. That is all most folks ever saw of Arizona. Very few travelers ventured out of their way to travel up north to visit Gordon's villages at Hopi.

Gordon stayed at the back of the Shell station convenience store by the restrooms, hidden by the racks of postcards and maps, hoping to line up a trick or hustle some cash. He had to keep out of sight of the clerks, who knew him all too well, and would bounce him outta there as soon as they spotted him.

Today was not starting out too well, though. He saw his uncle's pickup parked at the pumps. Gordon had not seen his uncle drive up, so didn't know where he was as he was not at the truck right now. Gordon decided on a quick exit and a short hike to the next gas station. But just as he was leaving, a hand reached out and grabbed his shoulder.

"Nephew."

He turned and wrenched free of his uncle and tried to flee, but Uncle Wallace was even quicker and took him again by the arm.

"You don't skip out on me, young man." Wallace turned him around and took him firmly by both shoulders. "Your ma been worried sick. Come on, I'm taking you back with me. Get in the truck." Wallace dragged him toward the truck at the pump, opened the door, and forced him into the passenger seat. But Gordon, faster than a dust devil, scampered across the seat, and without even opening the door, fell forward through the open driver's window and shot off across the lot. Now Wallace was no match in speed with Gordon so he didn't even try to catch up to him. And, as he hadn't yet filled his tank, didn't try to drive after him either. He just threw his hands up in the air, uttered a Hopi curse, and pumped the gas.

Gordon had, unfortunately, left his backpack behind in the truck, and this was a real problem because the few possessions he had were in that pack. It had his jacket, necessary in the cool, high desert nights, even in summer. There was his toothbrush, his headband, his few changes of clothes, his knife, and most importantly his lucky totem—a hummingbird that he had carved out of cottonwood when he was ten. Fortunately, the few bucks he had managed to scrounge were still in his jeans pocket. He thought about how he might swipe a jacket and a new backpack at Conroy's down on Second Street.

Gordon wiped tears from his eyes as he headed back toward town, through the rusted cars in the scrap lot behind the Shell station. He couldn't count that Uncle Wallace wouldn't check out the various gas stations along I-40 looking for him, so he decided to skip hustling the other filling stations on I-40 today.

A scamper of ruby-throated hummingbirds flashed before Gordon and drew his attention toward a '55 Chevy with no engine but with a still intact back seat. He walked over and peered in. He looked around, and as no one was in sight, he crawled into the back seat. Because he'd only had a few winks of sleep this morning, he curled up, found a tarp on the floor, pulled that over him, and drifted off into a fitful sleep.

An eagle circled above the sheltered box canyon searching for rabbits. The high sun above his wing cast a fleeting shadow on the cornfield below. Three stalks of corn grew out of each of the many small mounds in the field. Squash vines crawled along the base of the corn, and beans corkscrewed their tendrils along the stalks of the corn, climbing upwards toward the sun. These three staples of the Hopi diet had fed generations. Spider Woman walked the field—a gourd in one hand, a bucket of water in the other. She carefully watered each mound, preserving every precious drop she could. The sun scattered prisms of light in the few renegade drops that did manage to escape the gourd between the bucket and the mound.

Far off on the horizon towering clouds were mounting with the promise of a summer storm. Lightning was streaking to the ground in spikes of thunder as the storm approached. Spider Woman looked up and began to chant and dance. The storm grew, filled the canyon, and began to splash life into the sucking, waiting cornfield.

Cheap Trick's eyes fluttered as he turned over in the back seat of the car, but he did not awaken.

☆☆☆

What? What was that? Cheap Trick looked around him—disoriented. He was outside the Chevy. It was early afternoon. Had he really slept that long? He walked through the scrap yard and onto a side street and past the alley where only last night he had given his third blowjob of the evening to some old crank. It looked so innocent in the daylight—just boxes, bins, and dumpsters, not the towering caverns of shadow and doom that they assumed at night.

He reached the main street—the sun still blinding him. He looked left. He looked right. He nodded and turned to the left, thinking he might cop a soda at the corner store where the cooler was in the back and out of sight of the clerk. He passed a yellow dog leashed to a parking meter—panting, and trying to squeeze into some shade by the fat base of a street lamp.

He walked into the air-conditioned store and headed to the back. He had just enough change for some Fritos if he could stick a cold soda down the back of his pants. As he walked down the chip aisle, he passed a young guy about his age. When he reached the Fritos, Cheap Trick looked back. The young man was staring at him and smiling. Cheap Trick nodded and returned the smile. The guy was a cute little blond twink. Cheap Trick wondered if the guy had any cash. He walked up to him.

"I'm Gordon." He held out his hand. He was never shy about introductions. They were what kept him alive on the street.

The young man was nervous and quickly looked away.

125

"Got a name?" Cheap Trick pushed and offered his hand again.

The guy looked back and took his hand. "Tom. I'm Tom."

"Got a cigarette?" Cheap Trick asked.

"Don't smoke. Sorry."

"Nah, that's okay." He studied the guy. "I'll give you a blowjob for five bucks. Or you can give me one for ten." Tom's eyes widened, and he looked around to see if anybody else had heard that. "There's an old car with a back seat just down the block. We could go there if you like."

Tom couldn't answer, but his eyes were nervously scanning the store. Cheap Trick was not about to waste any more time with some closet case loser who didn't know what he wanted, so he turned to go to the cooler. Tom reached out and touched Cheap Trick lightly on the shoulder. Cheap Trick turned back.

"How did you know?" Tom asked softly.

"Ah jeeze, when you been around as long as me, you get to know these things." He studied Tom. "Ever been with a guy before?" Tom shook his head and looked down. "Got any money?" Cheap Trick continued.

"Some."

Cheap Trick held out his hand, and Tom emptied his pocket. "Come on, let's get some eats and get out of here."

As they walked to the car, Tom kept staring at Cheap Trick. He was nervous but excited too. "You Indian?"

"Nope, I'm from England." Cheap Trick threw Tom a glance.

"You don't sound very English."

"Yeah, my dad's the Earl of London."

Tom looked at him askance with a sly grin. "Su-u-re."

"It's true. We got this really big estate on a hill by the river and everything. My mom's got this crown with all kinds of jewels and shit. I play on the river all day long. Got my own boat too, don't ya know?"

"Then how come you're here in this shit hole then?" Tom pushed back.

"I got kidnapped by ponies."

"You are so-o-o full of it..."

Cheap Trick gave Tom a punch on the arm and started running

126

down the side street toward the scrap yard and the Chevy. Tom ran after. They arrived at the car, both out of breath. Cheap Trick leaned back against the car, breathing hard. Tom stood before him and put his hands atop the car on either side of Cheap Trick's head as he looked into his eyes. Tom leaned forward and gently kissed him. Cheap Trick was startled. Not because of the kiss but because it was so tender. He had never experienced that before. He reacted by pushing Tom away, opening the car door, and pulling him into the back seat with him.

Now Cheap Trick was totally confused. He had never had sex like this before. It had always been furtive, quick, messy—emotionally painful. His whole inner being was opening like a squash blossom to the morning sun—sudden, fluid, rushing, sweet. He lay there with Tom's head on his shoulder. Tom was gently asleep. Cheap Trick reached over, put his hand on Tom's head, and stroked his hair, so blond and fine and clean smelling. Cheap Trick took in Tom's breath that smelled of clean linen or saddle leather. He closed his eyes as the sun had already set, but just before he nodded off to sleep, he looked up to find his star.

☆☆☆

What? What was that? Cheap Trick looked around him— disoriented. He was outside the Chevy. It was late afternoon. Had he really slept that long? He walked through the scrap yard and onto a side street and past the alley where only last night he had given his third blowjob of the evening to some old crank. It looked so innocent in the daylight—just boxes, bins, and dumpsters, not the towering caverns of shadow and doom that they assumed at night.

He reached the main street—the sun still blinding. He looked left. He looked right. He'd lost most of the afternoon and needed to cop some cash. So he turned right and headed down toward the bar that opened the earliest. He planned to hang out on the corner where the guys would drive by after work in their low riders, scrap heap pickups, or shiny late model sedans looking for a quickie before heading home to the wife and kiddies. They would drive really slow down the street, peering out of the passenger window, turn into the side street and wait for Cheap Trick to walk over to the car, lean in the passenger window, and say hi. Cheap

Trick knew all the cops in town so he didn't even bother to ask if the john was law anymore.

He felt bad about his backpack, but knew his uncle would keep it for him till he got back to Hopi. He was just concerned about how he would get through the night without his jacket, but there wasn't time to raid Compton's or go dumpster diving. He needed cash for food right now.

Most of the guys who came cruising by would be regulars. He knew how much each one would be willing to pay. Some were so cheap he would just give them the finger and wave for them to go on their way. And the first couple of drive-bys were, indeed, regulars. One just waved hello but drove on. The second was a notorious drunk who was only interested in a line of drinks this afternoon and parked and went straight into the bar, mumbling to himself and scratching his ass.

Then a green van with tinted windows cruised by. Cheap Trick didn't recognize it, but it slowed down slightly as it passed and then drove on. Cheap Trick watched it go down the block, turn right at the next intersection, and come back again, having made a circle around the block. It slowed again as it passed. Cheap Trick smiled and gave a little wave. This was a potential new customer, and it was good to be on best behavior, at least the first time. The van drove on, though; turned left this time at the corner and disappeared. Cheap Trick shrugged, figuring the guy wasn't interested, and was already on the lookout for the next customer.

But two minutes later the van reappeared and pulled up at the curb. The window slid silently down, and from the dark interior, a hand reached forward with a fifty-dollar bill—five times his usual top dollar rate. The hand waved the bill, and Cheap Trick walked up to the window.

"Got change?" A voice echoed from the interior of the van.

Cheap Trick stepped back—*cheapskate, prick tease.*

"Just kidding." The voice chuckled. "Come back."

Cheap Trick walked back to the window. He tried to peer inside but could only see the outline of a dark figure with reflecting aviator glasses.

"What do you do?" the voice asked.

"Depends," Cheap Trick answered.

"What will fifty get me?"

"Most anything. But ya gotta use condoms."

"Okay, hop in."

Cheap Trick glanced around the street. It was quiet. The sun was already making illuminated lace of the trees as it began to set west of town. He stepped up to the cab, swung into the seat, and shut the door. The driver activated the door locks, put the van in gear, and set off down the street.

"Got a name?" the stranger asked.

"Danger," Cheap Trick replied.

"Really. Then I'd better be careful, huh?"

"Where we going?"

"Down the road a bit," he answered, as they passed the city limit sign and headed out toward the desert.

"You gonna bring me back? I ain't got no way to get round other."

"Sure. I'll take ya wherever ya wanna go."

They drove on in silence. The driver kept glancing over at Cheap Trick and began to play with himself.

"Kinda hot. Why don't you take off that shirt?"

"I'm fine." He glanced over quickly toward the driver and then turned back and stared out the passenger window.

"For fifty bucks you can take your shirt off, okay?"

Cheap Trick slipped off his shirt and laid it in his lap. They continued to drive on. By now, all remnants of Winslow had long disappeared, and Cheap Trick was beginning to get nervous.

"I didn't sign on for no trip to the moon here. Where you taking me?"

"Not far." The driver was looking hard at Cheap Trick now. "Let's see what you got there."

"What?"

"Take it out. You cut or uncut?"

"Uncut."

"Mmmmm." The driver pushed on. "Come on, let's see it."

Cheap Trick began to unbuckle his belt and open his jeans. Just then, the driver turned onto a dirt road that was hidden by a row of cottonwoods. It was almost dark now, and the van's headlight beams

129

jumped and swayed as the van plowed slowly down the pitted road. Up ahead was a house surrounded by even darker trees. No lights. The van pulled up behind the house and stopped. The van was still. The headlights extinguished.

Later, the van pulled out of the side road on to the road from Winslow going away from town, deeper into the desert. There was no moon. The van drove along the deserted road with only its parking lights on. It turned off the road by a bridge and down into an arroyo and drove till it was out of sight of the highway. Not long after, the van returned. It climbed back onto the highway and headed out to the interstate toward LA.

By a salt cedar at the edge of the arroyo, a dark shape almost blended into the bank of the dry river. There were no flowers. There were no clowns. Only a face half covered by a hubcap, with just one sightless eye pointing toward a certain star.

☆☆☆

What? What was that? Gordon sat up. He looked around him— disoriented. He threw the tarp off and climbed out of the Chevy. It was already afternoon. Had he really slept that long? He walked through the scrap yard and onto a side street and past the alley where only last night he had given his third blowjob of the evening to some old crank. It looked so innocent in the daylight—just boxes, bins, and dumpsters, not the towering caverns of shadow and doom that they assumed at night.

He reached the main street. The sun sent shimmering waves off the asphalt. He looked left. He looked right. A hummingbird zoomed out of the sun, paused before him and then darted left off down the street, stopping to hover over a yellow dog leashed to a parking meter.

Midnight Clear

There was a seam on the roadway crossing the bridge, such that when a car passed over, it sent a *thump thump* echoing underneath. When it was busy during the day, the *thump thumps* came frequently, overlapping and creating a thunder that echoed along the riverbank. During the night, the sound came infrequently and accented the stillness.

It was going to be a very cold Christmas Eve—with the scent of snow already in the air—and there had been a few flurries as the afternoon gathered into dusk before the clutch of night took its frigid hold.

Rainbow and Gal were huddled around their meager fire, kept alive by scavenging the riverbank for anything that would burn—hopefully through the entire night. Their few belongings were stacked up like sandbags around a foxhole to help keep out the needles of icy wind. The tips of their fingers poked out through worn gloves as they fumbled with a dented pot to heat water so they could use the damaged Ramen Noodle Soup packet scrounged from a dumpster behind the 7–Eleven. Maybe Gal would wait till midnight to give Rainbow his gift—a short flask of brandy that Gal had saved for from a week of panhandling when Rainbow wasn't around.

In country, the coppers flew overhead like crazy-wheeling drunks—*thump thump, thump thump*. Rainbow was Corporal Edward Declan Connelly—Boston Irish. So raw he still thought they were fighting the enemy for the good of the country. He was called Rainbow because he was *that* way. His best and only buddy was Gal—short for Gallagher but also because he was perceived to be Rainbow's *gal*. They had soon found each other despite the monsoons, the mud, the lousy food, the blood, the moans, the endless boredom, and the constant rain of shells—*thump thump, thump thump*. They managed, however, to get away together

131

now and then for half an hour, hidden amongst the sacks of flour in the storeroom behind the mess. Time so precious and ever so brief, their hearts—*thump thump, thump thump.*

After the slaughter was over, and they were shipped home and dumped on the streets of LA, they stayed together. Somewhat broken, keenly cunning, resourceful as two feral cats, together they opened a shop repairing typewriters and small business machines. Then came the computer. They struggled, tried to adapt, created more debt to stay afloat, and finally had to flee in the dead of night in their broken-down Pontiac to the Rocky Mountain west. Their car barely made it across the Continental Divide—*thump thump.*

They never completely recovered. Too many demons. Too much alcohol. Inner wounds too tender. But they stayed together through it all. There was never one without the other through many decades, many journeys, many disappointments.

☆☆☆

"Deck, oh Deck. I can't believe you're still abed. And this being Christmas morning and all." His mother called him Deck, not Eddie. But he didn't want to stir. The room was cold—the covers warm, scooched up tight around his head, cradling his ear. Only his susceptible eyes and nose were exposed to the bite from the window slightly ajar. He promised he'd get up at the count of ten. "Eight, nine, nine and a half, nine and three quarters…"

☆☆☆

"Soup's ready." Gal offered Rainbow the watery, soft noodles.
"Thanks."

It was dark now. The fire glowed and sputtered. Gal put on a few more pieces of wood from a broken table someone had tossed onto the riverbank rather than take to the dump. They ate in silence.

Thump thump. Rainbow's mind wandered to the sleeper car his family was taking to Chicago to visit his grandmother; snuggled in his berth, eyes almost closed. *Thump thump.* The sound of the train lulled him toward sleep. *Thump thump.* He always watched for that moment when waking turns into sleep like a snake gliding silently into water. But he could never quite grasp it—it always just slipped away. *Thump thump, thump thump.*

Gal always cooked. Rainbow always cleaned—tonight taking their few bowls and cooking pot down to the stream to wash up. With tonight's cold, it was hard to find any running water, and Rainbow had to hack at some ice to find the little trickle to serve his need. Though poor and without much provision, they were both meticulous about keeping clean—their persons and their possessions. Rainbow carefully rinsed the pot and bowls and climbed back up the bank to their shelter under the bridge. He stored the utensils and scooted up close to Gal, sitting by the fire.

"Here, let me warm you," Gal whispered as he straddled Rainbow from behind, wrapping his blanket around the both of them. He reached into his pocket and pulled out his gift. "I know it's not quite Christmas yet but thought you could use this now." He opened the brandy and handed it to Rainbow. Rainbow bowed his head in gratitude and offered the first sip to Gal.

They sat like that for some time, drinking quietly, the cars overhead passing less often now. *Thump...thump.*

Rainbow was the first to notice the child—six, maybe seven. The way the boy stood at the edge of the bridge it looked as though he was lit from within, but of course, Rainbow thought, it had to be the play of the streetlight against the ice reflecting up from the river below.

"Gal..." Rainbow breathed so softly it could hardly be heard. Gal looked up and saw the child now holding out both his hands filled with Christmas cookies.

"For you," the child said softly.

☆☆☆

Eddie continued his countdown, "Nine, nine and a half, nine and three quarters. Nine and seven-eighths..."

"Edward Declan Connelly, I am *not* going to call you again," his mother boomed from the kitchen.

"Oh boy, she means business now." Eddie knew that for sure. And for just a minute longer he savored the warmth of the covers trying to drag him back into sleep. But then he could smell the wafting scents of Christmas—oatmeal, apples, cinnamon, brown sugar. And there were tangerines, coffee, and bacon sizzling on the stove. He bounded up and out of bed, shut tight the window, and still in his pajamas with the fuzzy feet, faced the light pouring through the door and quietly walked toward his mother.

☆☆☆

The police cruiser was parked on the bridge, the lights blinking and swirling. *Thump thump.* Two officers were responding to a call from a pedestrian who believed he had spotted something suspicious under the bridge. The officers scrambled down the riverbank and peered. It was dim and hard to see. There were the remains of a fire still smoldering, sending up curls of smoke like lazy spirits going home. And there, huddled together and covered with a thin blanket, were the bodies of two men locked in a tight embrace, drifted snow cradling their faces.

"Oh jeeze," one of the officers commented. "Looks like we got ourselves a couple of stiffs. Better call it in."

The second officer stared uncomfortably at the bodies. "Will you look at that," he said. "Two guys in each other's arms. So desperate to keep warm they had to resort to that." *Thump thump.*

Miss Charlotte's Jump Rope

Miss Charlotte was one hundred and three years old and in no mood to be fussed over—ever. Lino was flustering around her once again, like a startled canary in a cage, prodding Charlotte to take her nasty vitamins. And Charlotte had no mind to oblige.

That Charlotte was considered difficult by the staff would be an understatement. She would *demand* to go faster as she was pushed in her wheelchair, brandishing her cane like a saber as she led the cavalry charge into the dining hall or rec room.

She reigned at the head of the best dining table by the window and commented, in no uncertain terms, on the manners (or lack thereof) of each timid soul unfortunate enough to have no place else to sit for luncheon except at *her* table. Their lunch was always brief, avoiding eye contact, and inviting certain indigestion as they scarfed down their chicken tetrazzini and mystery berry cobbler, scurrying away as quickly as possible after.

Miss Charlotte came from a very distinguished south Alabama family whose wealth came from lumber. They resided in a small town supported mostly by timber harvesting and her family's sawmill. They lived in a classic antebellum country house, with a wide two-story front porch supported by sturdy Doric columns. Some of the domestic help lived in what had once been slave quarters, built far enough away from the main house so the stench of the unwashed would not impinge upon the delicate nostrils of the fine ladies.

Charlotte was an only child and especially beloved of her father, Graydon Shelby Jackson, who delighted in giving piggyback rides and showering frilly frocks on his rather spoiled baby girl. She was particularly delighted with the bracelet of glass beads Grandmother Jackson had given her, and she would dance around the azaleas holding her wrist up to the sun to watch the sparkles shoot off in jeweled rainbows. To her they were crown jewels. And she never quite recovered from being that little princess.

Lino struggled. From a family of six boys and two girls, and the next to the youngest, he was the runt of the family. He was described as delicate—thin, with fine features. He was from a Hispanic family, and his five brothers were either crack athletes or tending toward the rough and tumble. His sisters thought he was a wimp. His father barely spoke to him. His mother was so frazzled most of the time, with such a rambunctious family, that she rarely had time to give him much thought either. With little education, and deep inner torments, he found a job as a personal attendant at Winston Manor, "a secluded but active community of gentle men and women in their golden years" (or so said the brochure) in Reseda, California. While not an institution from a Dickens novel, it could hardly be described as a premier pleasure palace either.

Charlotte could not abide most of the personal attendants. She became testy when they tried to dress her, and she absolutely forbid to let anyone tend to her hair except Lino. For some reason he seemed to soothe her. His gentle hands fluttered around her head like a cloud of butterflies, and before she knew it, she was once again presentable. She would turn to him with her sweet princess smile and pat his hand, like a dried spotted leaf falling from an autumn branch.

He would lead her to the window where she could look out over the back of the property to the line of trees bordering the Ventura freeway. There was always a little sun there in the mornings, even in winter. She particularly liked the way the sun dazzled her glass bead bracelet as she drifted in and out of remembrance of her lost Alabama home. She would doze off till Lino revived her by reading from Jane Austen. *Pride and Prejudice* was her favorite, and she never seemed to tire of hearing it over and over.

The other guests resented that Charlotte could command so much of Lino's time when there were so few personal attendants to go around, but they would be firmly reminded that she was a hundred and three, and by far the senior resident. Allowances, after all, must be made.

Lino always dressed in white scrubs, looking like the center pole in a collapsed circus tent as the scrubs always seemed far too loose on him. Perhaps they did not have his size, or maybe even the smallest size was too roomy for his slight frame. He had his long hair pulled back in a tight ponytail, accentuating, even more, his delicate features.

He took great pride in his meticulous attentions to Miss Charlotte. He felt he could be himself with her, unlike with the other staff and guests who tended to instinctively shun him, or even worse, taunt him. He would move like a ghost through the hallways as he tried to blend into the surroundings and disappear during his duties of the day. But in Charlotte's room he felt safe. Her world of southern gentility soothed him and let him feel fleeting moments of peace.

She had resided at Winston Manor almost twenty years now, and her room was full of southern charm. She had the oak dresser that had graced her bedroom as a child and over it, the faded photo portrait of her parents, stiff and glassy-eyed. Her mother had died shortly after the photo was taken, during the Spanish influenza epidemic of 1918, leaving Charlotte grief-stricken at eleven. The metal institutional bed was covered with a family chenille bedspread, worn but still quite respectable.

This morning it was finally warm enough for Lino to have the window open slightly, which let the early spring breeze billow the languid, sheer white curtains.

But there was something different about Lino today, Charlotte noted. Not that she paid much attention to his appearance generally. However, today she did notice something. What was it? Oh yes, Lino's hair was not constrained. No ponytail today. It fell loosely around his face as he leaned forward, almost obscuring it.

"Lino," she commented, as he dusted the figurines on her dresser, positioning the silver hairbrush and comb in their proper place. "Your hair."

"Yes. Do you like it?" He smiled shyly.

"Well, it's the first time I've seen it like that. What prompted the change today?"

Lino hesitated, briefly suspending his dusting. He thought for a moment and then came over and sat next to her at the window. She briefly imagined he might start reading to her again.

"Not sure if I should tell you," he confided.

"As you like." She smiled. "I'm not trying to pry."

He nodded then said, "Okay. I'll tell you, but no one else here in this shithole must know yet." He paused and bowed his head. "I'm transitioning. My hair this way is the first step."

"I don't understand." Charlotte was flustered by his graphic reference to Winston Manor. "First step to what?"

"To becoming a woman."

Charlotte became profoundly silent.

"You may call me Lina from now on, if you please."

Still Charlotte did not respond. Lina was disappointed. "I thought you might understand. Sorry if I offended you," she said with a modicum of bitterness.

"No. No. I'm not offended," Charlotte responded ever so softly.

Lina bent down and took Charlotte's hand. Charlotte looked up at Lina and seemed to see her for the first time. "Oh yes, I remember."

☆☆☆

Eight-year-old Charlotte knew there was going to be a problem with the jump rope her father had given her for her birthday. Here she was dressed for Sunday church and her crisp light-blue dress with the starched and layered petticoat was just too stiff and cumbersome to jump rope in. Why had Martha dressed her so-o-o early? It was still two hours before they would get in the buggy for the dreary ride to the Presbyterian church, and she was just itching to try out that fun-looking new present. Why did her birthday have to fall on a Sunday anyway, for heaven's sake? And even though it was only nine o'clock in the morning, she was already feeling the swamp heat and knew that by afternoon, when they returned, it would be a veritable bathtub of swelter.

Well then, there was nothing to do but try and find Otis and see if *he* had any brilliant ideas as to how to pass this miserable time till they left for church. She scampered back in the house with the new, still too stiff jump rope, crinkled from being folded up in the dry goods store, and dumped it on the kitchen table where Martha was fussing with the noon dinner. Charlotte could spy her birthday cake, hiding on the top shelf of the pantry.

"Not on this here table you don't," Martha scolded. Charlotte deposited the jump rope on the big sideboard with the set of white ironstone pitchers just waiting for the next batch of ice-cold lemonade.

"You seen Otis, Miss Martha?" Charlotte asked politely hoping for a real answer rather than a grunt and a "Shoo."

"He be off in dem woods, I do believe. Skee-daddled off outta here 'bout half hour go."

Charlotte danced to the swing door and looked out through the screen into the deep-breathing blackness of the pine woods that came up almost to the back of the house. She never liked going in there. She much preferred the sunny garden, with the swing set her father had constructed for her on her last birthday, backed by mountains of red and pink rhododendron.

Otis was eighteen—bragging that he was a full-fledged teenager and would soon be an adult. However, as his mama said, he was a little slow, and he enjoyed Charlotte's company more than kids his own age. Martha was his mama and kept him close by doing kitchen chores 'stead-a sending him out with the loggers. Mind you, that certainly suited him for sure. He was slight—small for his age, but handsome as a new pair of shoes. His hands were delicate and adept at fixin' things 'round the house. He would much rather play house with Charlotte in her playroom, or help with the taters, than go out with the workers to the forest or shoot cans off the fallen oak by the creek. His favorite thing, though, was to weave strings of ribbons and little flowers in Charlotte's hair on a day when it was raining, and they would sit up in the playroom by a toasty fire on a winter afternoon after lunch.

Otis was very light skinned compared to his mama. He used to say his daddy was probably some traveling carney, catching his momma by surprise behind the Ferris wheel, but Martha kept very private 'bout Otis's paternity. And it was very clear Martha was not going to say one more word on *that* subject. However, Charlotte noticed her father often stared intently at Otis when she and Otis were playing together.

Charlotte gazed into the depths of the dark woods, calculating how much time before church. Swallowing her distaste for the forest, she leaped off the back porch and scampered into the woods even before the screen door snapped shut. Martha looked up from kneading her bread with a *humph* and gave it a quarter turn before punching at it again.

Charlotte raced through the edge of the woods where the light still filtered in near the back of the house, but she slowed and proceeded cautiously as the light dimmed further along. She almost felt her way, weaving through the trees hand over hand till she saw a little clearing up ahead. She heard noises and thought it must be Otis. She slowed and proceeded forward quietly, thinking to jump out and give him a fright. But as she got closer she could see two figures. One was Otis, but she was not sure who the other one was. All she could see was that it was a large, solid man—perhaps one of Papa's sawmill workers.

Something tensed inside her, and she froze. She knew from some deep recess that she must not go forward. She peered from behind the scaly bark of a dark tree—hidden and silent. Otis was bent over, his arms stretched out before him supporting himself against a sentinel pine. His pants were down around his ankles. The other man was grasping Otis's shoulders and throwing his body up against Otis's backside. He was breathing heavy and squeaking strange, muffled sounds. Otis turned his head toward her. His eyes were closed, and a pained grin distorted his face. Suddenly he opened his eyes and saw her. He let out a deep sigh and startled Charlotte, who turned and fled back toward the house.

Martha looked up as the screen door slammed. She only saw a blue blur as Charlotte raced through the kitchen. She heard Charlotte bound up the massive main staircase and into her Daddy's library.

"Daddy, Daddy."

"What is it, Charlotte? You're not getting all fussed up before church now, are you?"

"Daddy, you have to come quick. Some man's hurting our Otis. Out back in the woods."

"What now? Otis in trouble?"

"Please, Daddy, come."

Graydon rose from his desk, followed Charlotte out of the library, down the staircase, and back through the kitchen. His eye caught Charlotte's new jump rope on the sideboard. He grabbed it up as he passed, thinking it might prove useful for giving a whipping if need be.

"Be there trouble, Mista Jackson?" Martha gleaned, with a sharp pang of dread, from the look on Graydon's face.

"Otis." He barked as he charged through the swing door and catapulted off the back stoop. Martha sprang after, wiping her hands on her apron and grabbing a knife from the kitchen table.

Graydon, Charlotte, and Martha slashed through the dark and damp of the forest—bracken and briars snagging at their legs.

"Where?" Graydon called out to Charlotte.

"The clearing. The light." She breathed heavily.

Two figures could now be seen up ahead. Graydon slowed his pace. He gripped the jump rope.

Martha called out, "Otis, baby!"

The two figures turned. Otis looked toward his mama as he pulled up his pants. The man turned away, pulling up his trousers, and started to lope away to the other side of the clearing.

"That you, Bo? What the...?"

Bo turned toward Graydon, his face flushed. Scrambling with his belt, Bo backed up slowly toward the edge of the clearing. Bo was Graydon's overseer at the mill. Graydon advanced toward him, slapping the jump rope against his leg.

"Twern't my fault, Mr. Jackson. That...that...boy...he seduced me. He be a witch boy for certain. I was just passing through. He come on to me. Not my fault. You can see that, can't you? Look at them eyes. That mouth. Trouble. Anyways trouble."

Graydon stopped and turned toward Otis.

Otis ran toward his mom. "We jus' playin' Mama." He fell in her arms, and she held him tight, dropping the knife that fell with a rustle to the forest floor. Martha stared at Graydon with a mix of horror and pleading.

Graydon turned to Bo and then to Otis and then back to Bo.

"I'm not the first. Just ask round. This boy bad trouble. He need be taught a good lesson." Pointing to the rope in Graydon's hand. "That rope there. That a lesson witch boy like him understand. Lesson to all temptation. Give it me."

Bo raced over to Graydon with surprising speed. He snatched the rope from his hand, pushing Graydon to the ground, and quickly whipping together a noose. He ran to Otis, grabbed him from Martha and dragged him to a tree with a low hanging but sturdy branch. He quickly swung the rope over the branch and fitted the noose over Otis's head, as Otis struggled with a look of terror in his eyes.

Charlotte cried out, "Daddy!" as she rushed to Graydon who was rising to stand again. She grabbed his hand and looked up at him, searching for his eyes. He refused to look at her. She started forward toward Bo and Otis. Graydon reached out and grabbed her by her church dress.

Martha fell to the ground, searching for the dropped knife. Bo gave a terrific yank on the rope, lifting Otis up in a sudden whoosh. Otis squirmed, legs flailing, his hands grasping at the rope around his neck, his eyes bulging, his face purple. Bo tied his end of the rope around the trunk of another tree and gave it another sharp tug.

Martha stood, and screaming, rushed at Bo, coming up quickly and driving the knife deeply into the soft, fleshy mound of Bo's neck, spurting a sudden gush of scarlet. He collapsed, spitting and gurgling. Otis hung still as washing on a cloudless morning—ticking gently back and forth like the pendulum in the grandfather clock on the stairway landing.

☆☆☆

The sun fell through the window onto Charlotte's hands. She fingered the sparkling glass beads on her now well-worn bracelet. She looked up at Lina who smiled sweetly at her, unaware of Charlotte's tumultuous memories. She raised her hand and brushed back the hair falling forward on Lina's face. She looked deeply into Lina's eyes, rimmed ever so lightly with liner. Charlotte slipped off the bracelet, clutching it in her hand. She reached out and took Lina's hand, pulling it toward her. She placed the bracelet in Lina's open hand and closed it around the beads.

"This is yours, my dear, in memory of a boy much like you. His name was Otis."

You Are a Winner!

Eight-year-old Gregory Jankowski lay on the floor with his chin resting on his hands, sprawled out in front of the wooden temple of sound. Before him, three pillars, masking the dark recesses of the fabric-covered speakers, rose in fluted columns to just below the pale, benign, glowing face of the dial. His eyes were half closed. His feet bobbed and swayed to the music. "Hi ho, Silver, away!" The music swelled and the drama began.

Each day had its ritual. And Gregory was like a strict stationmaster clocking train schedules. He knew every show on each day and its exact time. And he was as precise as a watchmaker as he found the bars on the dial that blared forth his favorite programs—*Sergeant Preston*, *The Inner Sanctum*, Jack Benny, Sam Spade, *The Thin Man*, Edgar Bergen and Charlie McCarthy, *The Shadow*. And the list went on and on.

Gregory's father was not at all pleased with this devotion to this frivolous entertainment. He wanted Gregory climbing trees, building forts, charging the enemy lines out of doors. He was disgusted with this sissy, artsy crap. He wanted to be building a *real* man. But his mother always intervened on Gregory's behalf. She stressed how necessary it was to stimulate the imagination of a growing child, and besides, the boy played outdoors all the time, as well. Of course, she neglected to say that the play was mostly with the girls who lived across the street. They adored letting Gregory be the cowboy hero—constantly saving them from fates worse than death. He used to ride his horse—a large abandoned trunk found in the alley and about to be picked up by the trash collectors. It was secreted to a hiding place behind the tool shed and dragged out with cries of "Come on, men!" whenever damsels needed to be rescued.

"Oh, Mother, please, please, pretty please," Gregory pleaded,

145

tugging at his mother's sleeve in a way he knew she could not resist, clinching the plea with his head resting mournfully on her shoulder. That should seal the deal for sure. The only ploy more appealing would be tears, but he was not about to stoop *that* low—unless absolutely necessary.

"So, I don't understand. What's this all about?" she finally enquired after much sleeve tugging.

"It's the Lone Ranger contest. First prize is an all-expense-paid trip for the whole family—that's you and me, and Bobbie and Dad. All of us—all paid—for a week to Hollywood to meet the Lone Ranger and Tonto. Just think what a treat for the whole family." He had no reservations now about applying his urgent *how can you resist me* look.

His mother sighed and weighed how she was going to explain this to Dad. But maybe she wouldn't need to. "Okay, what exactly do we have to do to enter this contest?"

Gregory smiled and became both animated and diplomatic. "I have to write a two hundred and fifty word essay on why I want to go to Hollywood. Then we need just ten Wheaties box tops and an official Lone Ranger entry form—which is on the back of each Wheaties box, but we only need just one of those."

"You've got to be kidding me. Ten boxes of cereal? Couldn't we buy just five and use the top and the bottom?" His mother was ever practical and thrifty.

"Oh, Mother, no. The tops and the bottoms are very different. That wouldn't work. I would certainly be disqualified"

"Well...I think there's one box in the pantry. And there might be another in the trash. You can take those two, and we can collect the rest over time as we use up the boxes."

Gregory began to panic. "No, no, no, no. You don't understand. There's a deadline. We *have* to send them in by the end of *this* month." *Okay, add pleading eyes, really convincingly—right now.* Gregory rose to his knees and took his mother by both of her shoulders, looking deeply into her eyes. "Mother, please, we need to buy at *least* eight more boxes of Wheaties this very afternoon."

His mother started to speak but hesitated.

Gregory went into hypermode. "I'll eat Wheaties every single day for breakfast and lunch till they are all gone. I promise. Think of all the money you'll save on peanut butter and jelly and other unnecessary groceries." Gregory now applied his *I am serious* stare and rested his case. He knew he had her.

"Oh, all right, then. But don't tell your father, understand?"

"Oh, Mommy, I love you so-o-o much." He kissed her and gave his award-winning smile.

As the trash had already been collected, nine more boxes of Wheaties were duly purchased—their box tops rendered up, and the stash of cereal boxes hidden away in the laundry room where Daddy never ventured except to get a screwdriver or a pair of pliers as he kept his tool box there. Mother counted on Dad never questioning why the endless supply of Wheaties boxes had no tops. She knew he was never very observant about mundane household matters.

Gregory worked diligently on his essay for days after school—a nub of pencil scratching out block letters on a sheet of ruled notebook paper; a fantasy about the delights of Hollywood, California and why he just *had* to go there. Then he carefully filled out the entry form, and counted out the box tops over and over again to be certain the count was accurate. He addressed the envelope and accompanied his mother to the post office to make sure the postage was sufficient. He even offered to pay the postage from his meager twenty-five cent per week allowance. But mother was generous, and paid for the postage herself.

But now came the agony of waiting for the announcement of the contest winners. It would be at least three months. How was he *ever* going to patiently wait that long to find out if he was the winner?

Now Bobbie, Gregory's elder brother by two years, was a star pitcher in Evansville's Dryer Little League. He was almost always found wearing some part of his baseball uniform on any particular day—except for church and Sunday dinner after. One day it might be his baseball shirt. Another day his pants or his red striped socks and cap. Dad was so proud. At least there was *one* real boy in the family. Bobbie constantly urged his father to catch as Bobbie practiced his pitching routines. Dad frequently urged Gregory to join them, but Gregory always had a convincing excuse—homework, an ingrown toenail, sniffles, or an urgent need to stack the firewood his father had grouched about for weeks last fall. But one Saturday there were just no more acceptable excuses. Dad had slipped on a ladder cleaning out the gutters and sprained his ankle—no way could he be catcher today. Now it was Gregory's duty to catch as Bobbie practiced his fastball.

Gregory assumed the catcher's stance—urged on and corrected by his father, who was temporarily leaning on his grandfather's borrowed cane.

"No, no. Crouch lower," Dad growled. Gregory complied. "Glove facing out. The pitch is going to come straight at you." Gregory was sweating. He just knew his face was about to be ripped clean off with the first pitch. "Head up. You got to be ready for the pitch." Already Gregory's legs were beginning to shake from the unfamiliar crouch position. He was beginning to get a cramp in his right leg. "Okay, now, Bobbie. Let him have it."

Bobbie wound up. His right arm poised for maximum thrust—his outside leg compensating for the juxtaposed arm. He eyed his target and let the ball fly with an urgent whoosh. The ball slammed toward Gregory. Now while Gregory was not exactly athletic, he *was* quick. And as soon as the pitch was launched, Gregory knew he had but *one* serious course of action. He fell forward on his face, arms outstretched as the ball whizzed over his head. He was not about to try to catch that nuclear missile.

"Ah, come on," Bobbie buzzed as the ball bounced across the lawn and into the alley. Dad was incredulous and for once speechless. Gregory was not about to give them a moment to collect themselves. He picked himself up, and raced down the street to the woods across the highway where he had a comfy hiding place in an old abandoned treehouse constructed by neighborhood kids a decade ago.

Gregory came trailing home just in time for dinner. His dad was so disgusted he didn't even speak to Gregory during the whole dinner. Bobbie had completely forgotten the incident and was rambling on about the Little League finals just two weeks away. The team believed they had a shot at the state title. Mother, previously apprised of the catching fiasco, managed to steer the rest of the dinner table conversation around to other, less controversial topics.

The subsequent months passed by in an agony of anticipation as the deadline neared for the announcement of the contest winners. Bobbie's Little League team had, indeed, won the state title and was now grooming for the nationals. Gregory saw this as a positive omen for his own success in the contest and was already planning what he would pack for his trip to Hollywood. Swim suit, of course—they would surely visit the Pacific Ocean in Santa Monica or Venice Beach or perhaps even manage a trip to Laguna Beach. (Gregory had studied the map of California with the intensity of Magellan charting his circumnavigation of the globe.) And of course, shorts, T-shirts, and sunglasses. Even though it would be winter in Indiana, it would *always* be summer in sunny Hollywood.

Then the day finally came. *The Lone Ranger* program promised they would announce the contest winners on the program this very afternoon. Gregory was stretched out in front of the radio—his hearing so sensitive he could hear the tubes humming in the growling bowels of the radio's intestines. For once, he could not endure the trivial exploits of the Lone Ranger and Tonto. All he wanted to hear was who had won the trip to Hollywood. And then finally…The announcer came on before the final credits.

"Ladies and gentlemen, boys and girls. I know you have all been waiting breathlessly for the announcement of the winners in our Lone Ranger Trip to Hollywood contest. And I am now proud and pleased to announce our Grand Prize winner is…" Gregory's heart stopped and his breath ceased. "Rachel Marquette of Baton Rouge, Louisiana. Congratulations, Rachel." Gregory finally took a breath.

Mother had been listening along with Gregory. "Sorry, honey." She put her hand on Gregory's shoulder. Tears welled up. But the announcer continued.

"But that's not all, boy and girls. We have additional winners to announce as well. Stand by till after this brief commercial announcement. Wheaties—breakfast of champions…" The announcer continued, but Gregory did not hear the rest. Maybe the judges had been

149

so enchanted with his essay that they had decided to grant a second trip to Hollywood. He was certain that was the case.

Finally the announcer returned. "Now then, I am pleased to give you our additional winners. First, we have two runners-up. Nathaniel Bradbury of Cleveland, Ohio, and Betty Jane Laughton of Wenatchee, Washington."

Gregory was once again thrown into utter despair. But then...

"And finally our three consolation prizes go to Donald Brazer, Cathy Campbell, and Gregory Jankowski. Congratulations to you all. You will be receiving your prizes within the next three weeks by US mail."

"Oh honey. You see, you *are* a winner."

"But what's the prize? He didn't say. Do you suppose it's a *weekend* trip to Hollywood?"

"Oh, I doubt it. It's only a consolation prize. I wouldn't expect too much, dear."

Suddenly Gregory brightened. "I'll bet it's a gun and holster, or at the very least, one of the Lone Ranger's personally autographed hats. Or even one of Tonto's headbands. That would be just so great, don't you think?"

Every day after the first week, Gregory rushed home and asked about the mail. Had his prize arrived yet? And every day he was answered with a "No, dear" But then the inevitable happened. He rushed home, and his mother was out shopping. What would he do until she returned home? He passed through the dining room on his way to the kitchen for a snack, when he suddenly froze. There on the dining room table was a parcel. He approached it, almost afraid to look. Yes! there it was—for him. He picked it up and read the label. It was postmarked Hollywood, California, with the return address of The Abbot Studios. Gregory tore into the wrapping. Inside was a box printed with a Capitol Sports logo. Gregory opened the box and pulled out...a football.

Gregory used a word he had never used before, although he had heard his father repeat it many times before. "Oh fuck!"

Magdalena—A Remembrance

Memory is fickle. It haunts us, teases us, and eludes us all at the same time. It can shape-shift—just when we think we have captured the essence of a memory, it can morph or merge with other memories and become a unique construct of our imagination. Or it is like a fun house mirror, so distorted that it never lets us see the true reflection.

But since we know that truth is relative, the best we can hope for is to present our own truth—from our own unique and personal perspective. Forgive me Magdalena if I have, by following *my* truth, not fully captured *yours*.

☆☆☆

Newly arrived in San Francisco in 1973, my partner, Orlando, and I found immediate refuge—with friends of New York friends—in a hippie house at the corner of Haight and Ashbury. Although the residents of this hippie house were mostly straight, there was no negative reaction to us as a couple. After all, San Francisco was rapidly becoming *the* gay Mecca of the United States.

Our actual *room* was a large closet with a mattress on the floor, and a window that looked out onto a ventilation shaft. Our adjacent roommate had *his* closet lined with egg cartons nailed to the walls to serve as a primal scream chamber. Needless to say, we wanted to find our own apartment as soon as possible.

One of our housemates had come across a vacant, furnished apartment on the top floor of an old Victorian on Fell Street, along the panhandle of Golden Gate Park. It did not suit him, so he told us about it, thinking we might be interested. We eagerly went to see it. But it was more like a finished-off attic than an actual apartment. It ran the length

151

of the house—the living room and bedroom had pitched walls matching the outside pitch of the roof. There was a tiny kitchen, a primitive bathroom, and a stairwell to the floor below. But it would suit us just fine.

Orlando wanted to take the apartment right away at only $150 a month with a $50 deposit. I was less certain, however, because we had just arrived from New York City and did not yet have real jobs—and only a small amount of savings. But his ardent faith in the abundance of the universe persuaded me to take the leap of faith that would be necessary for us to move out of our closet and into our very own sparsely furnished top floor.

We were moving our few meager possessions from the hippie house into our long, narrow apartment. I was approaching our stairwell with the last box when I heard a *psssst* from a doorway on the floor just below ours. I looked over. A diminutive lady with a red wig was waving at me. "You—you come," she whispered. I set the box down on our stairs and ventured over. She opened the door and I went inside.

She lived in an apartment on the second floor. Her front room had a large Victorian style, corner bay window, with a view of the street and park. Originally, this had been a single-family house, which had been subdivided into apartments. Behind her living room was a second room, with only an archway separating the two, and she had her bed in this second room, sheltered by a series of freestanding folding screens. Opposite the bed, her dressing table was in a second bay window at the side of the house, overlooking another Victorian house next-door, which had been converted into a Russian Orthodox church.

"You just move in?" she asked, with a thick Russian accent.

"Yes, Orlando, my boyfriend, and I. Hi, I'm Jerry."

"Oh, then that funny girl upstairs is gone, yes?"

"I guess so. It's just the two of us up there now."

"Oh, I'm so glad. She was always very rude."

"And what is your name?" I asked.

"Magdalena...Kolokolava. I am Russian," she said with a great deal of pride.

She led me further into the room. She looked to be in her late sixties or early seventies, was no more than five feet tall, and she walked with a cane. The walls were covered in Russian icons. Some looked old and were probably very valuable. There was a cleared oasis on one side of the room with a couch, an overstuffed chair, a lamp, and a TV set; but everywhere else, the room was filled with cardboard boxes, trunks, and dozens of plastic trash bags bulging with lumpy, unknown objects.

"I want to ask you a question." She leaned forward and pulled at my sleeve.

"Okay." I complied.

"Are you interested in making money?"

Oops, what have we got here? The thought flashed through my mind. *Not interested in any hanky panky, lady.*

"I certainly *am* interested. What have you got in mind?" I finally answered, being the perfect gentleman that I was—especially to little old ladies.

"I get money from the county for my disability. I need assistance every day and they will pay you $150 a month. Just a couple hours work a day. Are you interested?"

It seemed the universe was kicking in after all.

"I would love to help you. What exactly do you need me to do?" I was thrilled that we would be able to cover our rent. Orlando, a dancer, had already arranged to teach some dance and movement workshops, and his fees would probably cover the rest of our modest expenses.

"I cannot walk too good. I was a nurse and was attacked by the Black Panthers at a bus stop on my way to work at the hospital very early one morning. The doctors pronounced me dead, and as I floated above my body, I looked down and could see one young doctor continuing to work on me. He opened me up and massaged my heart, and I went *boom* back into my body. Just like that—*boom!*" She clapped her hands together. "Such a lot of pain. But he saved my life. That is why I am disabled. I can't work. The county gives me assistance. And I need you to help me a little each morning. Some mornings I need cleaning. Sometimes we go to the supermarket, the bank, or the post office. And I need help preparing food."

"I have an idea, then," I spoke up. "Orlando and I cook for ourselves each evening. We could make extra food and bring you down a plate when we eat. It's good. We're great cooks. Is there anything you don't eat?"

"Oh that sounds wonderful. Yes, that would be very nice. No fresh spinach. No baloney. No Brussels sprouts."

"When do you want me to start? We could bring your first dinner down tomorrow evening, if that suits you."

"Yes, yes." She went over to her dressing table behind the screens and came back with a bank envelope. "Here, this is for you for the first month. And I will give you money for food too." She went to her purse and took out twenty dollars. "Let me know when this runs out. And buy yourself a sweetie. Can you come down tomorrow at ten? I need to go to the market. You come with me. Okay, okay?"

"Ten o'clock it shall be. See you then."

I went upstairs and did a little *thank you universe* dance.

☆☆☆

I arrived at ten o'clock on the dot the next morning, ready to take Magdalena to the supermarket on Turk Street, which was only a few blocks away.

"Knock, knock," I announced as I poked my head in her front door.

"Yes, yes, come in," she directed, calling me into her boudoir, where she was at her dressing table. "Come sit with me. Come on," she urged. I entered, and pulled up a chair next to her. Behind the screens, and next to her bed, were stacks of trunks, more cardboard boxes, piles of old *San Francisco Chronicle*s, glossy magazines, hatboxes, and cloth-covered boxes tied with large, silk ribbons.

"Here." She scrabbled around in a bowl on her dressing table and pulled out a key. "Just let yourself in. Good to have for emergency too. I'm not too well you know. The doctor opened my heart, and now I have heart problems. Have to take many medyecins," she said with her Russian accent.

"I understand. Thanks. Good to have the key. I can let myself in to bring your supper too."

"Here, let's make a list for the store." She handed me a pencil and the back of an envelope. "I need tissues, makeup—gotta see what's on sale. I need Fourth of July cards for my daughter, my granddaughter, and my doctors. I need bread and crackers. I need medyecins—these need to be refilled." She shoved a half-dozen medicine bottles toward me to write down on the list. "I need cereal and milk. Maybe more, but that's all I can think of right now."

She then began applying her eye shadow and then her lipstick. She had somehow lost the art of a straight line, or even a gentle curve, and she blinked and bumbled her way through the haphazard makeup applications. This took at least fifteen minutes. During this episode, she regaled me with her history.

"My father was a Russian doctor, but we lived in China. My husband was Russian too, but we met and married in China. He was captured by the Japanese during World War Two and held as a prisoner of war. I never saw him again. When the Communists took over China, my daughter and I, we were forced to leave. We had two choices—go to Australia or go Brazil. We go Brazil. But always I wanted to come to America. I raise daughter all by myself. I was a dancer. See that?" She pointed to a garment hanging from one of the bedroom screens in a plastic dry cleaning bag. It was more like a coat than a dress. It was composed of highly ornate Chinese gold cloth with sparkles and long sleeves.

"I did exotic dance. Very classical—very Russian—very Chinese. I danced and danced. Men threw many moneyees at me. I keep it all to come to America."

She had put on a skullcap, made from old panty hose, over her thin, pasty hair, and fastened it with bobby pins. Then she positioned the red wig atop her head. The wig was so cheap it looked like a motel carpet. Then on top of that went the hat—a round pillbox with a veil, which she pulled down over her face to become Marlene Dietrich in *Shanghai Express*. All she lacked was a blood-red camellia and a ruff of black feathers.

"My coat." She gestured toward a ratty, grease-spotted, blue wool coat on a chair next to her dressing table. I brought it over, resisting the temptation to first shake it out a window to release any mice or old bird nests. I helped her into it.

"Okay, we go now." She rose, took her cane and her handbag, and was ready to start out the door.

"Ah Magdalena, aren't you forgetting something?" I pointed out as gently as I could.

"What?"

"Shoes."

"Oh," she exclaimed with a hoot and a laugh. "See, that's why I need you. The doctor opened up my heart, you know, and now I cannot remember anyeething."

It took us forty-five minutes to walk the few blocks to the store. She had to stop every few yards to catch her breath. For me, my first radical lesson in patience.

When we arrived at the store, I was not allowed to quickly run around picking up what was needed on her list in my very focused and efficient manner. No, I had to go with her while *she* picked out each and every single item by herself. And, of course, each cereal box had to be examined and the labels read, like she was one of the American Founding Fathers examining the Constitution for imprecise words.

Then welcome to the makeup aisle. Each sale item was fingered, removed from the shelf, turned over several times, and selected or replaced. Lipstick shades were compared like Michelangelo choosing colors for the Sistine Chapel. Cuticle remover, cotton balls, Q-tips, eye shadow, false lashes, and adhesive were collected and placed carefully in the shopping cart as if she was collecting uncooked Easter eggs.

Then we had to wait in cracked plastic chairs while her prescriptions were refilled. No, we couldn't go about the store on the other errands and just come back to pick up the medyecins when they were ready. No, we had to sit and wait, along with a line of junkies, hungering for their methadone fixes. She asked me to remind her to pick up an additional card for the pharmacist when we selected the greeting cards—the last item on her list.

I never knew there were so-o-o many greeting cards for the Fourth of July. Each one had to be opened, read aloud, and considered in great detail. And only then were the winners selected for each recipient on her list.

But not only did we need to select cards for each member of the family, all her doctors and nurses, *and* the pharmacist, but we also needed to get additional birthday cards, graduation cards, get well cards, and bereavement cards in case some of her friends at the senior center suddenly kicked the bucket before her next visit to the supermarket.

Then *finally,* we were at the checkout counter. Coins were carefully counted out, *after* each bill had been placed on the counter one at a time. The glaring looks from those impatient folks standing in the line behind us signaled imminent mutiny.

Finally, we were able to leave the grocery. And as a special treat we got to take a taxi back to the house. After all, we now had shopping bags to carry.

The whole morning consisted of four hours, of which I was being paid for two. But I was not going to complain. After all, every day could not be like this one. Right?

☆☆☆

Orlando and I carefully plated up Magdalena's meal each evening, and I took it down to her at six thirty. I would let myself in with the key and sometimes, when she was napping, I would leave the plate in her little pocket kitchen. She would place the empty plate for me outside her door when she was finished, and I would pick it up before going to bed.

The days went by simply enough. Some days the work was short. A quick clean, or perhaps I'd help her read and understand her mail as even with glasses she couldn't see very well any more. Government form letters were always a puzzle to her. And then there were the shopping days, which were always lengthy, labored, and very tedious. I was earning s-o-o-o many Heavenly Brownie Points. I was becoming the Olympic Champion of Patience.

Then one morning when I arrived, Magdalena was all a-bustle. She had a very special project for us that day. She went once a month to a local senior center to tell fortunes—as a Russian gypsy. Today was the day to prepare the fortunes. She had a stack of index cards and a stack of horoscopes that she had cut out of the daily newspaper. She had me

157

separate the individual horoscopes from each column, and regardless of which sign was represented, she had me paste each one onto an index card until the card was filled up. Then we would cut up the card, separating all the individually pasted horoscopes, and she put them into a cloth bag she kept especially for that purpose.

When she did her routine at the senior center, she would put on a record of Russian gypsy music and dance her very classical, very Russian, very Chinese dance extravaganza. And when she was finished, she would have each senior select a piece of index card out of her bag, and then Magdalena would read their fortune aloud to them. This she did every month, and that was the highlight of her otherwise simple and restricted life. Somehow, the fact that the doctor had opened her heart did not seem to matter to her all that much at these times.

When I left her that morning she was in a state of high excitement and urged me to be early the next morning, as the taxi was coming for her at nine thirty, and she had to be all made up, dressed, and ready to go long before that.

So the next morning I arrived at eight o'clock. She was already at her dressing table, wrestling with the transformation from little old lady to exotic gypsy. She was wearing a long, full, red skirt; an intricately embroidered, white peasant blouse; a floral fringed shawl tied around her waist, and a silk paisley kerchief tied tightly behind her head. And finally, a large, single gold earring dangled from her left ear.

She saw me come in, and leaped from the dressing table, twirling around in circles, without her cane, in Romany pirouettes.

"You like? You like Magdalena—the Russian gypsy princess?"

"Charming. Disarming. An unstoppable force of nature," I exclaimed, while somewhat apprehensive that she might also take a tumble. But her years as a dancer did not desert her, and she flowed across the room, her eyes shining, and a huge smile enlivening her face.

She was ready long before the taxi arrived. She put on her coat and checked her bag three or four times to make certain that she had not forgotten her little bag of fortunes. She re-examined her makeup and finally had me escort her downstairs to the street where we were to wait for the taxi.

"Oh thank you so very much," she smiled and patted my hand as I helped her into the back seat of the cab. She waved, as the cab sped off for the no more than five-minute ride to the senior center and her, once again, gala performance.

☆☆☆

It was Magdalena's birthday, and we were to celebrate with a party in our apartment with Miss K as the guest of honor. She refused to let me help her dress for the party that evening. She wanted her appearance to be a surprise.

Orlando and I baked a birthday cake, and planned a special Russian meal of borscht, pirozhki —a delicacy from a local Russian bakery—and a salad.

From our kitchen, we could look down upon, and through, a window of the Russian church next door. San Francisco had a large Russian population, and besides the numerous small churches scattered throughout the city, there was a major Russian Cathedral out west on Geary Boulevard. Magdalena very much wanted me to take her to a service there one day. This would be a special adventure, as it was not something she could do by herself any more. So most weeks she attended the church next door. And that is one reason why she had chosen her apartment—to be next to the church.

Often we would look down through the open church window in the summer and catch a service underway—with the wonderful singing, the swinging incense burners, and the ringing handbells accentuating the stages of the service.

Magdalena had become more open and playful with Orlando and I as she got to know us better. She loved to surprise us with little gifts and, of course, greeting cards for every imaginable holiday, Russian saint's day, or even a graduation celebration for the daughter of one of her doctors.

She was in gay spirits as Orlando escorted her up the stairs to our apartment this evening. To mark the special birthday occasion, she was dressed in a floral silk dress, a necklace of paste diamonds, and a matching tiara atop a blonde wig. I was busy in the kitchen finishing up the borscht that would be served before the pirozhki.

Orlando took her into our living room where we had a table set with some flowers, candles, wine, and a couple of silly presents that were nicely wrapped—each with a greeting card, which we knew she would like. He got her comfortably seated, and we began serving dinner immediately, as we knew she went to bed early, and we didn't want to overtire her with a late night.

She was delighted when we presented her with the birthday cake. And after having had a few glasses of wine during dinner, she had become mellow, contemplative, and a little sad. Orlando asked her about her daughter, Elaina.

"Where does she live?" Orlando asked. "Do you see her often?"

Magdalena hesitated before speaking. It was clear to me that this was a delicate subject, painful for her to talk about.

"She lives in San Bruno," Magdalena said. "She *wants* to come visit, but she has a daughter, and it's very difficult for her to get away."

"Just down the peninsula. That's not too far. Then do you go visit her?" Orlando followed up.

Magdalena pursed her lips several times before answering. "Not able to travel that far."

"Do you have any pictures of your daughter and granddaughter?" Orlando asked, trying to show his interest and raise her spirits.

"I'll show you sometime," she answered. "But they are very old pictures."

"That's okay. You can show us when you want." I tried to divert the conversation as I knew her daughter's indifference was painful to her.

"I think it's present time, don't you?" I asked cheerily. Magdalena's eyes lit up, and with her Betty Boop lips, she gave each of us a kiss on the cheek. "You are such nice boys. But you don't look like brothers," she twinkled.

"Oh Magdalena, we're not brothers. I've told you that. Look at us. Orlando is very dark and from Paraguay. And I am blond and from Cincinnati. How could we be brothers?" I teased back.

"Oh yes, I know. This is San Francisco. I watch television. My doctor is like that too, you know. But to me you are cute little brothers."

I had another birthday surprise for her besides the wrapped presents. "Magdalena, as your very special birthday treat," I offered, leaning in closer, "I'm going to take you to the Russian Cathedral on any day and time of your choosing."

Her eyes lit up, and she clapped her hands together in great delight. "*Spasiba, spasiba!*"

☆☆☆

A visit to the Russian Holy Virgin Cathedral for Magdalena was like a visit to Mecca for a Muslim. This was an important event to be prepared for weeks in advance. She booked the taxi three weeks ahead of our departure. She bought a new wig that took us an hour to pick out at the beauty supply store, and she dug deeply into her Chinese trunk looking for the special lace shawl with which to cover her head in the Presence.

The day finally arrived, and she made sure I was dressed in at least a shirt and tie, as I did not own a suit or sport jacket. She had packed a bag with oranges and apples for sustenance. With those, she packed a container of wipes, hand cream, sunglasses, a map, lipstick, nail polish, blush, hairspray, scissors, two spoons, a water bottle, and a toothbrush. One had to be well prepared for a pilgrimage to face the Lord.

When I came down to pick her up, she was seated on the sofa, completely dressed, the mantle over her head, white lace gloves on her hands, and the fully packed bag beside her on the floor, handbag in her lap.

"I guess there's no need to ask if *you* are ready," I said, perhaps a little unkindly.

"I called the taxi to make sure it would be here on time. The service is at twelve."

"But the taxi is coming at ten. I'm sure we will arrive in plenty of time. Early even."

She tusked at me. It was nine thirty. "Let's go down now."

"Isn't it a bit early? There's no place for you to sit downstairs. Won't you get tired standing that long?" I pleaded with her to wait in the apartment a bit longer.

"No, we go now. He'll just go away if we are not there waiting for him."

"Oookaaay." I offered my arm, and she took it. I carried the bag, and she carried her cane and purse.

She offered me an apple and an orange in the cab as we whisked down Geary.

"I think I'm fine for now, but thanks," I said, refusing the offering.

Within minutes, we pulled up to the cathedral with its gold onion domes, and large Russian Orthodox cross over the entrance. We went inside.

Being a novice to the Orthodox tradition, I was unaware that the congregation stood during the service. I had no idea how Magdalena could endure standing that long. And we still had an hour and a half to wait before the service started. I scrounged around the side rooms and found a folding chair for Magdalena to use until the service began. She was reluctant to sit, until I told her she could stand for the service itself, but until then she would be all right in the eyes of the Lord if she needed to sit.

"How you know what Orthodox Jesus say is all right?" she scolded but sat anyway.

During the wait, she pointed out the various aspects of the cathedral and the elements of the Russian service. This was all new to this very Presbyterian, Ohio boy.

The service itself was mysterious, uplifting, and very oriental. It was sensuous and spiritual at the same time. I so enjoyed watching Magdalena as she was carried away with rapture during the ceremony. She stood the whole time, and her eyes gleamed with adoration.

I could tell she was exhausted when we finally got back to the house. She said she wanted to take a little rest, and I helped her get out of her church clothes, and she got comfy in a bathrobe. She lay down on her bed, and I put a blanket over her. I tiptoed out and let her rest.

That evening, when I brought down her dinner, there was a note taped to the outside of her door saying she had gone to bed for the night and wouldn't need supper.

☆☆☆

Then it was gypsy time again! How quickly the month had passed. Even though we had dozens of fortunes left over from the last event, we had to start all over again from scratch and make new ones. That took up one whole morning. Then the clothes had to be laid out for the next day. The wig needed grooming. Yes, this time the gypsy would have blonde hair. And finally the bag had to be pre-packed with Labor Day cards for all the seniors—I didn't know Labor Day even *had* cards. And then there was the bag of fortunes, apples and oranges, nail polish, hand cream, touchup makeup, and layers of an archeological dig that descended layer by layer to the bottom of the bag.

Again, she had me come down long before she needed to be escorted to the taxi.

"For you," she said, as she put the phonograph needle on the record of gypsy music. She then twirled around the living room, radiant, graceful, and looking no more than eighteen. This month she had made some castanets out of metal lids from small pickle jars—tied them together, and fastened them to her fingers with dental floss.

I took her to the taxi, made sure she was comfortable, and waved good-bye as she sped off, once again, to delight the seniors. It was curtain time.

☆☆☆

I came back upstairs with Magdalena's dinner later that same evening. Orlando was just serving up our dinner.

"She's not there," I said, concerned, when I returned.

"Probably dozens of encores," Orlando joked.

"No, it's not like her. I'm worried."

"Maybe they invited her to stay on for dinner at the center."

"No, she would have called us."

"So what do you want to do?" Orlando asked.

"Should we call the police?"

"I guess. Or maybe the hospitals?"

"I know. I'll call Kevin." I picked up the phone.

Kevin was our landlord. He lived with his family in Oakland. He was an orderly at Saint Francis Memorial Hospital, and always very solicitous about Magdalena's well-being. He would know what to do.

"Hi, Kevin, it's Jerry."

"How's it going?" Kevin replied.

"We're worried about Magdalena. She didn't come back from the senior center this afternoon. Quite unlike her. She's always home by midafternoon. Just took down her dinner and she's still not there. Not sure how to find out where she is. Any ideas?"

"Want me to call around the hospitals?" he asked.

"Yeah, could you do that, please? You probably know best who to talk to."

"Will do. I'll let you know what I find out. Bye."

Later that evening Kevin called back. "I'm sorry, Jerry. Magdalena suffered a massive heart attack while she was dancing. They took her to SF General. She didn't make it."

"Oh Kevin..." I turned to look at Orlando, and he knew immediately what had happened.

"Now, don't you worry about a thing. I'll take care of notifying the daughter," Kevin offered. "And Magdalena advised me when she moved in that she had donated her body to the hospital for research. So guess there won't be any funeral to arrange."

"Is there anything you want me to do at the apartment?" I asked.

"Not tonight. I'll come over there tomorrow, and we can look around together and figure out what needs to be done."

I turned to Orlando, "Well, she went doing what she loved—another star in the firmament."

"Another gypsy in the sky with diamonds."

☆☆☆

And then finally the daughter *did* come to her mother's apartment for a visit. She took all the icons, a few other valuables, and split without saying hello, good-bye, or thank you very much to anyone. She consigned the rest of Magdalena's possessions to the trash. Kevin and I were left to clear it all out and clean up. Some things went to the

Goodwill, but most went to the dumpster. Kevin very generously offered to pay me for my time and help. And after all was removed, he hired me again to repaint the apartment for a new tenant.

Finally, when I was done with the job, I stood in the middle of the empty apartment and looked around. There was not a single trace left of Magdalena. No gypsy music—no flashing Chinese gowns—no paste diamond tiaras—no gypsy shawls—no pickle jar castanets. Just the lingering memories.

Paseo

Even though the breeze was softly pressing off the Mexican Caribbean, the sweet and pungent aromas of grilled pork, onions, and pineapple from the taco stand drifted down across the small plaza to where George Brightman sat on a low wall in the shade of palm trees, gazing out across the water to Cozumel, just as the ferry was pulling up to the Playa del Carmen pier. George admired the Caribbean Sea's bright and distinct layers of color—a large, wide band of turquoise stretching out from the edge of the beach; further out, a smaller, darker band of cobalt blue; and finally a thin ribbon of aquamarine at the horizon.

Several groups of children were playing on the beach. In one group, a young girl with pinned-up hair—in a one-piece pink bathing suit with dancing elephants—was shoveling white sand and flinging it at her younger brother who had a swimsuit that sagged at the butt; probably full of sand. Their mother sat in an aluminum folding-chair with a bowed seat that looked about to give way at any moment. She was slathering on lotion, shaded by a *palapa* and chatting on her cell phone—completely oblivious to the carnage her children were creating.

George was a neat, plump little man in his late fifties; balding and in shorts—unable to disguise his flounder-white legs that still had rings where his tight socks had left permanent marks from years of office work. George was, however, in a kind of trance today. This was one of those rare, perfect moments for him. The sun was warm this early April afternoon, but not blistering. The palm fronds, sounding like whispering baskets, waved gently above him in the just perfect breeze coming off the sea.

The aromas from the taco stand. The sound of the children echoing up from the beach below. The *paseo* of citizens going about their business: carrying plastic bags of groceries from the market; talking on

167

cell phones; corralling kids from tearing off to the beach. The tourists wandering from the Cozumel ferry in straw hats the size of small planets. George sat there taking it all in. He closed his eyes and thought he would never leave. He wanted to capture this moment and keep it forever sharp, like a snow globe capturing the swirling snow around the Eiffel Tower or the Empire State Building.

He had just come from lunch at the other end of Playa del Carmen. He'd enjoyed a cold Bohemia beer and shrimp tacos with melted cheese and an assortment of salsas at his favorite little restaurant back from the beach, La Cueva del Chango—Cave of the Monkey—a handmade dome with the bottoms of wine bottles cemented into the roof of the structure to allow soft light to filter into the interior. The sides of the structure were open to the elements and sunlight reflected off a plantation of banana leaves to give the interior a submarine shimmer. One expected to see coral fans with angelfish sampling the salsa. A small pond and fountain graced the interior. Behind, a Yucatan jungle created another patio environment. He had thought at that moment that it just couldn't get any better, but he paid his bill and walked La Quinta Avenida and then along the beach to the older part of Playacar to the old plaza by the beach where he sat now. He had nothing else to do this afternoon, and he just loved that. He had been vacationing alone for the past ten days and would be returning tomorrow to Des Moines; and now he just wanted to savor every last moment of his all-too-brief vacation.

Even though he had just eaten, he kept eyeing the grandmotherly vendors selling cups of fresh fruit, looking as beautiful as they looked tasty. Spears of mango, watermelon, pineapple, cucumber, jicama, stuffed into tall plastic cups and sprinkled with red chili powder when served—an assortment of exotic birds-of-paradise made from fruit. He could stand it no longer and wandered over to the vendors' carts. The ladies were peeling fruit and cutting it up on small cutting boards that sat on large inverted plastic tubs. He ordered a mixture of pineapple and mango with the red chili and went back to his perch on the wall. He sat there, his legs crossed, nibbling on a spear of pineapple and watching the show unfold around him.

George prided himself in "knowing people" and so loved to make up little scenarios about the people he watched as they passed by. "There, that couple coming this way..." he commented to himself as a young couple approached. "Lovers," he mused. They were animated as they passed by, gesticulating wildly. And though George's Spanish was adequate to order a *café con leche,* he was somewhat uncertain as to the context of their present conversation which he heard as they passed by. He caught something about cards and flowers. "Oh yes, that's it— planning their wedding. Obviously she wants to spend a whole lot more than he does." He smiled to himself. "Oh dear, this is going to lead to many heated arguments further along in their obviously very passionate marriage. Hope the sex makes up for it." He giggled.

☆ ☆ ☆

Marie-Louise and her brother Germaine had just come from their parents' newspaper and magazine shop. It was barely larger than a closet, but with the addition of candy and gum and a few plastic toys that kids loved added to the mix, their parents managed to squeak out a living. Of course, it was a six-day-a-week job, with only Sundays off for mass and maybe a stroll on the beach before a big meal with the family that lasted most of the afternoon.

Marie-Louise was *not* going to let Germaine bully her into letting him use her credit card again. "No—absolutely not," she insisted.

"And who got you that card? If it hadn't been for me working at the bank, you would never have gotten it."

"*Claro.* But it is I who pay for the damn thing. Last time I let you use it you spent a fortune on flowers for Carmalita. Oh, Carmalita, my darling. My beloved, Carmal-i-i-ita."

Marie-Louise noticed the gringo sitting on the wall eyeing them as they passed by, going all native by eating his mango out of a plastic cup. Too creepy. She much preferred the summer when it was hot and rainy, and there were fewer tourists and she could go about her life without being ogled by old lechers. "And did you ever pay me back for those flowers? No. Never! Jerk."

"But I will. You know I'm good for it."

She threw her hands up in the air as they walked on and out of sight.

☆☆☆

George licked the last of the red chili off his fingers and tried to clean them on the fragile little paper napkin that shredded in his hands. He looked around for a drinking fountain where he might rinse off. There was none. So he licked his fingers like a grooming cat.

Just then a nice breeze lifted up over the plaza, and George once more closed his eyes and drifted off into one of his Mexican holiday dreams. But he was jarred back into the present by a loud masonry power saw not too far away. He had seen workmen constructing a balustrade earlier, but they must have taken a lunch break and were now back at the racket of construction. He looked over, hoping it would be but a momentary distraction from his Mayan Riviera reverie.

There were three workmen. They were covered in stone dust and cement. Their dark hair was dusted with a coating of powdered sugar. Their heads looked like little Mexican wedding cakes. George was inclined to study them for a moment and once again use his powers of observation to construct an amusing story about these three.

Obviously the one on the left, with a broken nose and way too bushy eyebrows, was a drug dealer. George named him Carlos. The next one, Jorge, was short and compact—no doubt a wrestler who doubled as a bank robber on weekends. And the third—who looked like a Roberto— was tall and rather handsome and for sure ran a stable of *chicas* for the *turistas*.

God, he was good at this, George prided himself. He sat back, stretched out his feet, and wiggled his toes to loosen the sand he'd accumulated walking on the beach in his sandals earlier.

☆☆☆

George's "Carlos"—though his real name was Antonio—was carefully examining the plans laid out before him next to where the tall and handsome Edelmiro was laying the just cut stone that would form a foundation for a pillar of the balustrade.

"Why do you have to leave before the weekend?" Edelmiro whispered to Antonio. "Your classes don't start till Monday. We could have the whole weekend together. My aunt is going to Cancún to visit my grandmother and will be gone till Tuesday. I have the place to myself. We could have the whole weekend together."

Antonio shook his head. "You know I promised to spend the weekend with my father. I didn't see him at all during Christmas."

"But I won't get to see you again till June."

"Come visit me at the university. My room is small but we could cuddle up nicely." Antonio gave Edelmiro a big smile.

"Hey, will you two *maricónes* get your asses over here and help me with this?" Piero called out to them as he struggled to lift the next stone up to the saw.

"What's the matter, your wife sap all your strength this morning tapping that tiny dick of yours?" Antonio jibbed as he and Edelmiro rushed over to lend a hand.

"Tiny, yeah sure. Comes down almost to my knee."

"You must have very high knees," Edelmiro joked as they lifted the slab up to the saw bed.

☆☆☆

George had been watching this exchange and concluded that the whispering was the finalization of a plot to extort a widow in Cancún. He wondered if he should alert the authorities, but decided against it when he realized he would be leaving tomorrow and would be unable to attend any trial as a witness. Best not to get involved, he concluded.

The last of the tourists from the docked ferry were straggling off the pier, some passing by George as he continued to lounge on the low wall, still shaded by the nearby trees.

Playa del Carmen seemed to attract many more Europeans than Americans George had observed. Just now, a family was approaching, speaking Italian. The faces of the two young girls and an older boy were hidden by floppy sun hats. The girls were carrying bags with flippers and snorkels. The boy was showing off his yo-yo skills. The two girls were pulling toward the beach but the mother and father had them firmly in hand and resisted their impulse.

The father was in his forties—tall, almost abnormally thin, wiry, and tan. He wore a Speedo swimsuit with an open Hawaiian shirt and huaraches. He was smoking as though he was on his way to meet Anita Ekberg. George named him Paolo. His wife he dubbed Donatella. She was younger than Paolo and slightly on the fleshy side—probably a superb cook. His mouth watered, thinking of her homemade lamb lasagna. He was certain she had her own garden with at least six different kinds of tomatoes and three varieties of eggplants. She had on dark sunglasses, as large as Cinemascope, a scarf and a sun hat. She looked like Sophia Loren ducking into a limo. She wore a sarong-like dress and platform shoes. She obviously was not that enamored of the sun.

George decided that Paolo had a mistress in Verona who played the cello in a symphony orchestra, and could talk for hours on end about archeology and Chinese porcelain. He was sure Donatella loved to sew and read movie magazines. He imagined the girls braiding each other's hair under a pepper tree and the boy climbing the tree and tossing cherry pits down on the girls to annoy them.

☆☆☆

Actually this time he was not *too* far off the mark as to his speculations. Except that Paolo was named Gianfranco and was the owner of a winery in Lombardy. He hadn't performed sexually in fifteen years since he was involved in a motorcycle accident that crushed his testicles. While his sister, Chiara, was a ceramic artist in Puglia, and these were her husband's children by a previous marriage. Her husband did all the cooking and she couldn't even keep a plastic plant alive. Yeah—pretty close.

☆☆☆

George was very pleased with himself. He had had such a splendid lunch, a charming stroll, and a delightful afternoon exercising his acute powers of observation. However, the sun had shifted, and he was no longer as shaded as he had been previously, and he was starting to get a little too much sun for his fair skin. Also, his book was calling him, and he was contemplating a nap and perhaps an ice cream on his way back to the hotel. He had discovered, and become addicted to, a mango sorbet from a little shop on a side street. And he was already planning where he might dine this evening. He was thinking to go once again to his favorite taco restaurant on Avenida Constituyentes.

But then a shadow passed over him as he realized he would be heading to the airport way too early the next morning. He would barely have time for his favorite Yucatan breakfast, *huevos motuleños*—a tortilla with fried egg and banana, ham and peas smothered in tomato sauce and melted cheese—in the hotel's rooftop restaurant with the morning breeze nudging sweetly off the sea. Then he would have to scurry to the cab with his tightly packed carry-on, wearing trousers, his pinching socks, and a long-sleeve shirt to shield him from the air-conditioning on the plane.

Reluctantly, he rose from his perch on the wall and looked wistfully around at the passing scene: the ferry pulling out from the pier into the crystal waters toward Cozumel; the teenagers texting; the families trudging up from the beach, the kids too red and too tired. He gave a nod to the fruit ladies and started off toward his hotel.

☆☆☆

An elderly Mexican couple was sitting on a bench, shaded by a fish restaurant, eating sliced papaya—their treat for the afternoon—when George passed by with his mango sorbet.

The woman commented, "You know, I feel so sorry for these pasty gringos with their little chicken legs, and their Father Christmas bellies. Look at that guy there. I bet anything he works in some overheated, over-air-conditioned office tower from eight till five every day. Then he goes home and microwaves a frozen dinner, opens a can of—what do they drink there?—Budweiser, and falls asleep before the news."

Her husband looked up with little interest and nodded his head. "Yes, I feel sorry for those people from first world countries." He nodded again, squeezed more lime on his papaya, and felt the breeze rising from the ocean, as the sun declined toward Mayan temples that slept peacefully, hidden by jungles with rainbows of parrots.

The Cure

"So what can I do for you *today*, Luther?"

Luther was really nervous. He had been pondering this for several weeks and had decided that today would indeed be the day to speak out. "I think...I think...well maybe...I like men," he replied in a soft voice, bracing himself for the certain lecture on perversion, psychosis, and hell and damnation. It had taken him three sessions before he could finally come out with this simple statement to his therapist.

There was a thoughtful pause. "Okay. So why are you here then? Is there a problem with that?"

Luther was shocked by this accepting response. He felt he had to speak out. "You bet there is. Hell, I mean...I wanna be *normal*." This was 1955 after all—what was the alternative?

"Okay then so how are you going to go about accomplishing that?"

Luther had to pause at that. What had it been? A month? Two? Was that all the time it was? He remembered it so clearly. Fern Lindkoff had actually accosted him in the stairwell backstage as he was leaving the men's dressing room. She had pushed up against him as he scrambled to escape her clutches, but she succeeded in forcing him into a corner and declared how much she was in love with him—and how could he not know what she felt for him? It was the closing night of a three-day run of a university production of *Suddenly Last Summer*. Luther had played Dr. John to Fern's Catherine—pretty hot stuff for a couple of sophomores. And they had played it to the hilt. Not to mention there is always a lot of camaraderie built up amongst the members of any cast that sweat through the rehearsals and the nerves of a first night together. And there are always a lot of warm, fuzzy feelings after the process ends and the show closes. Cast parties are notoriously maudlin.

Luther had had a good working relationship with Fern and they had joked and teased and worked hard on their parts together. But what was all this? He had no idea she felt this way. And what did he feel about her? Well he was flattered, that was one thing. She was sultry and much admired by a lot of the male cast and crew. She had a breathy, overripe quality, though, that smacked a little too much of a Marilyn Monroe wannabe. This was right after the movie, *Seven Year Itch,* came out, and a lot of the tight-sweatered co-eds were turning their heads toward the whistling boys, pouting, and saying, "What? Who me?" But to be honest, Luther was also feeling a great deal of panic right at this particular moment.

In his relationship with women, Luther pictured himself as an unassailable gentleman. His intentions were pure. His relationships with women were noble. In other words, he was scared shitless of them, and especially of anything that might even remotely smack of sex in any form.

"Oh Luther, say something," Fern pleaded, pressing her moist lips against his. Of course, a response was not possible as her fervent kissing impeded any reply. However, it did give Luther a moment to consider his options. Maybe this was exactly what he was looking for—an opportunity, with a not unattractive female, to break out of his increasingly uncomfortable shell. Maybe she would be just the one to set him free from his as yet unidentified fears.

Luther finally untangled himself from her advances and spoke up, "Yes, yes, Fern, I want this as much as you do. By all means let's date."

This was, perhaps, not exactly the passionate response she was hoping for, but it would suffice for now. She backed away, and holding hands, they gazed into each other's eyes as they headed off to the cast party, Luther's heart racing with he knew not what emotions.

☆☆☆

Luther and Fern dated—safely. Movies, study groups, dinners at the student union cafeteria, walks through the campus. Yawn. They even exchanged pens as a sign of their romance, although Luther had to surrender his very expensive Mont Blanc given to him by his grandmother as a graduation gift from high school. Fern offered up her

Bic.

Then one evening as Luther brought Fern back to her dorm in his car, she didn't open the door immediately, even though he had told her he *must* get back to study for a horrific exam on *Beowulf*.

Fern was more pouty than usual at their parting. She sat with her head drooped, breathing heavily—steaming up the car windows.

"Are you getting out or what?" he asked with a certain urgency.

She glared at him. "I don't understand," she finally spoke up.

"You don't understand what?" Luther responded, already having some idea what she might be getting at.

"Don't you love me?" she pleaded.

"Well...yes," Luther parried without a great deal of conviction and definitely not wanting to get into this right now.

"Then how come you never kiss me? How come we don't make out? What, are you some kind of a pansy?"

Woops. Now that was exactly what he did not want to hear or even contemplate. "Of course not. What an idea," he answered, valiantly defending himself.

Then the tears began to flow—recriminations, taunts, comparisons to a half-dozen other ever more aggressive ex-boyfriends. But Luther did not take her hand, did not seize her in a spasm of torrid passion, did not even bother to stop her effusive complaints. Instead, he sat with his hands folded, his head bowed, taking it all in and not protesting. Finally, Fern seemed spent. She turned and looked at Luther, gathered up her bag, and as she opened the door to get out of the car, she leaned over and said with a great deal of indignation, "I think I've made myself perfectly clear. I really see no further need for us to see each other, do you?" She waited for his protestation, but none came.

"Then can I have my Mont Blanc pen back, please?" Luther asked softly. Fern stared at him in stunned silence. "My grandmother gave it to me," he added pleadingly.

She reached into her bag, retrieved the pen, and threw it at him. "Fuck you, Bozo." She got out, slammed the car door, and retreated to the cozy comfort of her dorm room where she could commiserate with her girlfriends over hot chocolate and Lebkuchen.

That is when Luther decided he needed to seek some psychological counseling and made an appointment the next morning at the student health clinic.

☆☆☆

Luther had been assigned to a therapist named Nils Ellstrom, a Swedish psychology fellow at the university, volunteering some of his free time at the clinic. Luther had explained all about his predicament with Fern, and how he felt he needed some counseling. And Luther was now considering the question Nils had just asked him about how he planned to accomplish this leap to into aggressive heterosexuality.

"Well, that's why I came here. For you to cure me," Luther protested.

"I see. Well, you know, Luther, it really doesn't work that way. First, I see no problem with your liking guys. That's just the way it is. There is a graduated continuum between heterosexuality and homosexuality. Most of us fall at the heterosexual end, but there are gradations all the way down to the exclusively homosexual end. Perhaps you fall somewhere in the middle. What I think is, you should explore all of your feelings and find out exactly where you are along this line."

"No, no. That's not what *I* understand at all. Everyone says homosexuality is perverted and abnormal, and heterosexuality is what is normal. I want to be normal." Luther felt he had made his point and stood his ground.

"Okay then like I said before—how do you propose to accomplish that?"

Luther could see this guy was not going to just fix him. Nils kept putting the responsibility back on Luther. "Well then I guess I'll just go out there and try harder. Fern was probably not the right girl for me. I think the spark was only on her side. Think I kinda got caught up in her frantic enthusiasm."

"So have you got somebody else in mind?" Nils was being very accommodating and patient.

Luther thought perhaps an older, wiser woman might be just the right solution and was thinking of Hilda, a Dutch graduate student he had met in the drama department, though her principal field of study was anthropology. She was dark and smoky. She spoke English with a rich velvety accent, reminiscent of a mysterious Marlene Dietrich. They had shared some good laughs and a few intriguing discussions that wandered from the usual mundane topics he had had to endure from most of the younger students.

"Oh yes, her name is Hilda," Luther responded. "She's much more mature and worldly. We've had some great conversations, and I think she's interested in me as well."

"Well, that sounds promising. What do you propose to do?"

"Do?"

"You know, date? What kind of a date?"

"Ah, yes…A nice romantic dinner, I believe. I know a charming little Italian restaurant that is intimate and has great food."

"Sounds like a good start."

"And not too expensive," Luther added, wanting to end with a bit of levity. He was already feeling the pressure to perform for Nils.

"Well, let me know how it all works out then. See you next week."

"A date? Really? With me?" Hilda was surprised. She was thoughtful as she twirled a pencil between her fingers. Luther was afraid she might think he was too young for her.

"I know this really great restaurant. Think you'll really like it," he added to sweeten the proposition.

She looked up and smiled. "Sure, why not. When?"

"I was thinking Saturday. You like Italian, don't you?"

"Absolutely. Sounds perfect."

"I'll pick you up at seven." Luther knew this was going to be a great success. He would *prove* to Nils just how heterosexual he could be.

Luther pulled out the chair for Hilda. The restaurant was an Italian-American cliché. Red-checked table cloths. The requisite Chianti bottle covered with months of dripping candle wax. Breadsticks protruding out of a too-cute basket. A crepe paper poppy in a green bud vase.

"Isn't it charming?" Luther whispered to Hilda as he slid the chair gracefully under her as she sat down.

She looked up at him with a *you gotta be kidding me* look, but shook out her paper napkin and placed it on her lap. "Oh yes," she responded politely.

Luther sat opposite. He was very nervous, as he knew this date *totally* counted. He was already mentally preparing his report for Nils. He reached out to take Hilda's hand just as the waiter came over and offered them menus. Luther quickly picked up a breadstick to mask his previous intention. But he could not help but notice the very cute butt on the waiter, the bulge in the front of his trousers, and his dark, searching eyes.

"Ooo, the lasagna looks good. Want some antipasto first?" Luther asked, with exaggerated enthusiasm.

The waiter lingered. "Would you like to order some wine, sir?"

Luther looked at Hilda, who nodded in agreement. "What have you got?" she asked.

"We have carafes of house red or white. And I am very proud to say we have a very excellent Chianti for just a little extra," he added, pointing to the Chianti bottle in wicker wrap, dripping with candle wax.

Hilda wrinkled her nose slightly, "Nothing else? Don't you have any Pinot Grigio?"

"I'm sorry ma'am, but I have no idea what that is," the poor waiter fumbled.

Hilda sighed. She glanced at Luther. "The Chianti, then?"

Luther nodded to the waiter. "That will be fine. And two glasses, please."

"Of course, *signore*."

Hilda gazed around the restaurant with its Mount Vesuvius and Pompeii murals, obviously painted by someone who was more accustomed to painting supermarket sale banners than lush Italian landscapes, "Have you ever been to Italy?" she asked.

"I've not been abroad yet," Luther apologized, feeling vastly inadequate, and nibbling on his breadstick in self-defense.

"You would like it very much. The trattorias there are charming. Fabulous food prepared by little old grandmothers—the whole family involved with the cooking and serving." She paused. "Very different from what you find here in this country," she said, looking around the restaurant with obvious distaste.

Luther hesitated but leaned forward and whispered, "Would you rather go someplace else?"

Hilda realized she was being much too honest. She was shocked at her obvious rudeness and what might be perceived as snobbery. "Not at all. I *am* sorry. You must think I am a very poor guest. The lasagna and antipasto sound marvelous."

The food was, however, lavishly mediocre. The antipasto was out of a jar. The lasagna was dry. The wine was just east of vinegar, and the tiramisu was from a package and still frozen in the center. But Hilda was the soul of graciousness. She even allowed Luther to hold her hands and gaze into her eyes with great meaning, across the flickering candle just before it expired.

As they were leaving the restaurant, the waiter came over and opened the door for Hilda. "Thank you for coming, *signora*." He smiled and looked flirtatiously at Luther and said with extra meaning, "*Signore*, I hope I will see *you* again—very soon." A dagger of desire pierced Luther's gut, and he looked back and smiled at the waiter as they left the restaurant.

☆☆☆

"Well how did it go?" Donatella asked, as Hilda came into their apartment. Donatella came over with a snifter of good cognac, handing it to Hilda, and giving her a wet kiss on the cheek.

Hilda sighed, removed her coat, and snuggled up on the sofa next to Donatella. "The food was dreadful, but he's such a sweetheart—I just couldn't refuse him the date. He is so earnest and tries so hard to please, and he just stared at me with those big moony, cow eyes, trying way too hard to spark an impossible romance. But he is *such* a nancy boy. He has no idea...or well, maybe he does. I saw the look he gave the flirty waiter

181

as we left. I just hope he gets it together soon."

"Well, sweetie, you did your good deed for the year. Let's just hope you don't feel like rescuing any more lost puppies." Donatella scrunched up closer to Hilda and laid her head on Hilda's shoulder.

"Somebody is a little jealous," Hilda teased in a singsong fashion. "Huh? Huh?" She poked Donatella in the ribs in an attempt to tickle her.

"Well, maybe just a little." Donatella giggled.

"You have nothing to worry about."

"I know."

☆☆☆

"She's simply marvelous," Luther gushed.

"So it went well?" Nils made a few notes.

"I'll say."

"Did it lead to any sexual activity, like you'd hoped?"

Luther fidgeted. "Not yet, but I'm sure it will—real soon."

"I see. Tell me, did she seem receptive to you?"

"Oh yes, she could hardly keep her hands off me."

"That's nice. Did you kiss?"

Again, Luther felt he was lacking somewhat in Nils's expectations. "I felt it was too soon. I didn't want to rush her."

"But yet you said she could hardly keep her hands off you."

"Yeah, well, it's not quite that simple..."

"And how's that?"

"She's a real lady and..."

"Real ladies don't kiss?"

"Well..."

"Could it be that maybe *you* don't kiss real ladies?" Luther couldn't think of anything to say to that. "Are you going to see her again? Have you set up a second date?" Nils pressed on.

"No, I've left several messages, but so far she's not returned any of my calls."

☆☆☆

Gregory was a new graduate student in the drama department looking to land an MFA in theatre design. He had graduated from Columbia and had not yet made many new friends in the drama department. He was on the main stage of the theatre, contemplating his set plans for the upcoming production of *The Mikado*. He was singing, "A wandering minstrel I, a thing of shreds and patches…"

Luther was taking a shortcut through the theatre from his Restoration comedy seminar to his geology class. Every English major has to accrue at least some science credits. His head was down, and he was preoccupied with reviewing the chapter on igneous rocks that he had only skimmed previously. He prayed there would not be a pop quiz today.

"Hey there, pretty boy," Gregory called out to Luther from across the stage.

Luther looked up, flustered and blushing like a sunset. Gregory was wearing a bib denim overall and no shirt. He had a hammer in the strap at his side. He was also wearing a big smile. He had dark, shaggy hair that fell over his forehead and which he had to keep brushing aside. His smiling eyes were such a light blue they were almost invisible from a distance.

"What's the big hurry? Could you help a fella lift this ladder?"

It was as if Luther had been punched in the stomach. He'd never seen such beauty in a man before. "I…I got a class. Really gotta go, or I'll be late."

"Not a problem. You take care. Maybe I'll catch you again sometime."

"I could come back after class if you still need help."

"Yeah, why don't you do that? I'm Gregory, by the way." He gave a sly smile, a chuckle, and a wave.

"I'm Luther," he called out, rushing off to class, afraid even to look back, though he could feel Gregory's eyes on him until he left the stage.

☆☆☆

"Can't stand the student union food, can you?" Gregory asked as he and Luther charged across the quad in the first snowfall of the season.

"Guess it's all right. Never thought that much about it," Luther answered.

"Hey what say I take you to some place better for dinner tonight? Good home cooking. I know the owners. Real nice, and like family. And they really care about what they serve. My treat."

"Okay, I guess," Luther replied, trying to hide how pleased he was.

Gregory and Luther were inseparable. They studied together, ate together, worked on Gregory's sets together, and only reluctantly parted when it was time to go back to their separate dorms to sleep.

Luther had not been able to tell Nils about this new friendship. He was still waffling on about Hilda, and how he just *knew* it was going to work out any day now.

☆☆☆

It was only a simple student diner adjacent to the university. Luther had passed it almost every day on his way to class, but he had never even bothered to look at the menu in the window. Gregory led him inside, and they found a free table by a side window that was private and secluded.

"You gotta try the ratatouille. It's fantastic," Gregory enthused.

"The what? Rat pittuti?"

Gregory laughed. "No, no. Try it, I guarantee you'll like it."

"I don't know..."

Stelly, one of the owners, with her big grin, came over. "Hey Gregs, how's it hangin', doll?"

"Humpin' and thumpin'."

"You go."

"Whatcha got that's extra special yummy tonight?" Gregory smiled up at her.

"Oh hon, got stuffed cabbage to die for."

"Yeah give me that, and for my friend here let's have an order of your famous rat pittuti."

Stelly burst out laughing. "Okay, one rat pittuti and one stuffed cabbage coming right up. Drinks?"

"Got any of that Napa hooch hidden away in the back?"

Stelly gave a knowing nod. "Might be able to scrounge up something

184

drinkable you might like." She retreated to the kitchen.

"She's sumpin' else, huh?" Gregory grinned.

"She likes you," Luther commented shyly.

"And what about you, Luther?" Gregory tilted his head and leaned in toward Luther, trying to catch his eye directly. "You like me too, don't ya? Just a little? Huh? Don't ya? Huh, huh?" He leaned forward and chucked Luther under the chin.

Luther blushed. "Yeah, you're a great friend."

Gregory leaned back in his chair. "Ho, ho—just a great friend? Nothing more?"

"I...I don't know...maybe."

Gregory carefully studied Luther before launching into a subject they had never discussed before. He wasn't sure if it was the right time or not, but decided to just go ahead and jump right in the deep end. "You ever been with a guy before?"

Luther shook his head and couldn't look Gregory in the eye. Then he shyly asked, "Have you?"

"Yep."

"Oh."

"Shocked?"

"Maybe a little." He thought and then asked, "You been with a lotta guys?"

"Not too many. Mostly saving myself for just the right one."

"And how do you know when you've found the right one?" Luther looked up now, engaging Gregory's gaze directly.

"Think I already have."

Luther was sitting silently across from Nils's desk with just the faintest smile. Nils studied him intently. Something seemed different about Luther today. There was a new flavor of peace and serenity. He suspected something had happened. "How's it going with Hilda? Any new developments on that front? It sure has been a long time since you two started dating," he finally said.

Luther was shocked when Nils mentioned Hilda. He had nearly

forgotten about her. For a split second, he couldn't even remember who she was.

"Yes, something's happened—but not with Hilda."

"Oh really, do tell."

"I met somebody I really, really like."

"Oh yeah? And...?" Nils, smiling, leaned in closer to try and catch Luther's expression.

"But it's a guy..."

"Uh huh. And why am I not surprised at that?"

Luther blushed. "And I think we might be going to have sex."

"Well now. Isn't that just grand? I hope you guys have a really, really great time."

☆☆☆

And they did.

And Luther discovered that he was *definitely* at the far other end of the continuum.

The Opening

The last of the evening light softly illuminates the voluptuous petals of the waxy magnolia blossoms, making them look like they are being lit from within—white with a blush of peach overtones. Laura sits at her dressing table, staring out of the leaded bedroom windows of her Atlanta mansion at the magnificent tree as it shimmers like a regal ghost in the fading light. She turns to her mirror and fastens a freshly picked magnolia blossom above her left ear. She studies herself. A handsome woman in her early forties, she is dressing this evening for the erotic art opening at her gallery. She is dressed in a simple, tailored, gray dress with a black and silver leather belt. She struggles to fasten the clasp of a black onyx necklace around her neck. She sees her husband, Mark, looking at her through the bedroom door. He is dressed in a Valentino tuxedo and adjusts the cuffs of his shirt, but does not offer to help her with the clasp.

"Are you ready?" Laura asks.

"The car is here." He turns to leave.

Laura watches him disappear from her mirror.

The chauffeur, a handsome, dark Italian in his early twenties, dressed in a gray uniform, gray silk tie and a cap, leans against the limousine, smoking. The front door of the house opens, and Laura and Mark appear, ready to leave for the opening. The chauffeur snaps to attention and quickly extinguishes the cigarette. He opens the rear door for Mark and Laura to slip into the back seat. As Laura settles, she catches the chauffeur's eye, and he smiles discreetly. Laura quickly looks away. The driver gets into the car, adjusts the rear view mirror so he can watch Laura, and drives away.

Laura stares out of the passenger window. Mark looks out his window. The chauffeur tries to catch Laura's eye again, but she refuses to look up. They drive on in silence. Laura finally looks up and sees the driver staring at her. She catches his gaze for a brief moment but then leisurely looks away, refusing to take on any guilt for the moment of contact.

At the gallery, Randy, the caterer, is arranging a riotous bouquet at the food table. The servers are busy prepping and putting out the food, and the bartenders are opening bottles of wine and champagne. Behind the bar is a large painting of rare and imagined flowers. The bouquet spurts from an ejaculating phallus.

The limousine pulls up in front of Laura's gallery. A sign in the window announces the exhibit of Erotic Art, opening this evening. Laura and Mark emerge from the car. The driver tips his hand to his hat as Laura emerges. She does not acknowledge him.

The couple enters the gallery. The opening has not yet started. Mark immediately heads to the bar. Laura walks over to Randy as she surveys the room.

"Randy, the food looks wonderful, and the flowers are exquisite."

"Thank you." Randy reacts to her beauty and places his hand on her arm. "But not as exquisite as you are this evening, Laura."

Laura smiles coolly and withdraws her arm, turning to greet the first of the arriving guests.

The guests fall into two groups—the evening dress crowd—and the artsy crowd, more eccentrically dressed. It is an international evening, and one can catch conversations in German, Japanese, French, and English. As the guests file into the gallery, they first head directly to the food table or the bar, but as they pass through the gallery they sneak surreptitious glances at the erotic art, too embarrassed to address the art head-on until they have either a drink or a plate of food in their hands.

Laura is both cool and inviting at the same time. She is much admired in Atlanta art circles and seems to know everyone on a first name basis—patrons, artists, or press.

☆☆☆

There is a sculpture of a man and woman making love. However, it is somewhat abstract, and a couple are examining the artwork, trying to figure out who is doing what to whom, and what part belongs to which body. As the couple examines the work, they go through considerable contortions themselves, trying to make sense of it. They end up looking rather like the sculpture itself.

A young punk girl with spiked, bright-red hair approaches a larger than life rubber sculpture of a limp penis. A sign says *Touch Me*. She smiles and tentatively touches it. It begins to rise accompanied by some rather strange sounds. It rises to full erection, and then there is the sound of an explosion, and it begins to recede and become flaccid again with the sound of a sweet sigh. She reacts with some surprise, amusement, and embarrassment. She races to fetch her girlfriend, and they try it again together. It goes through its little show, and they collapse into a frenzy of cascading giggles.

In another section of the gallery, a collection of provocatively dressed, very realistic mannequins is huddled together in a close group. A number of guests stand around studying them. It is very difficult to tell the mannequins from the guests. A man cannot resist the temptation and reaches forward to touch one of the sculptures, not quite believing it can't be real. Next to him a woman, also mesmerized by the reality of the exhibit, reaches over and squeezes the breast of another of the figures. However, it is a real woman, and she reacts with shock and surprise. The woman committing the offense is thoroughly embarrassed and profusely apologizes to the startled woman. They both see the humor in it and begin to laugh.

Mark observes Laura engaged with her clients and leans in toward a young woman studying a multibreasted Earth Mother statue.

189

"Etruscan, I would surmise," Mark comments.

"What?" The young woman turns toward Mark.

"Very early art from the ancient world. Earth Mother often depicted with many breasts. Meant to promote abundance—healthy harvests—all that sort of thing."

"Rachel," the woman says, offering her hand.

"Mark."

"It certainly is a relief to know women like that existed only in ancient times. I would not like to be outfitted with all those appendages today," she smiles coyly.

☆☆☆

Two lesbians are walking casually through the gallery. They come upon a marble statue of a phallus. They pause for a moment, examining the artwork. They look at each other with mild disgust and walk on.

☆☆☆

Roland Blaze, art critic for *The Register,* is accompanied by Cash, his much younger protégé. Laura passes by, nodding to Roland as she passes.

Cash smiles at her and turns to Roland. "Who is that gorgeous woman?"

"That, my dear, is Laura, the gallery owner. Affectionately known in the art world as the Ice Queen."

"Oh really? And why is that?" Cash asks, staring after her.

"Because, my child, as far as we know, no one has ever been able to melt that arctic heart of hers."

☆☆☆

The artist, Stephan Brook, is standing with a couple who are examining his abstract, non-subjective painting.

The husband turns to Stephan and asks, "How do you figure this is erotic art? I don't see anything erotic about it."

"It's called *Libido in Santa Fe.*"

The husband seems unconvinced. "Hmm."

Stephan, pushing for a sale, continues, "You see, the explosion of red coming, as it were, into the yellow expresses the latent fear and loathing that the modern male feels for the post-feminist female."

The husband and wife step back to consider the painting more carefully.

The wife pauses for a moment and then says, after great consideration, "I don't know, honey. I think that libidos in Santa Fe have more green."

Laura has a brief moment between chatting with guests. She grabs a glass of champagne and scouts the room for Mark. She sees him chatting with the attractive younger woman who is holding onto his arm and smiling. Laura pauses and then turns away.

☆☆☆

A handsome young man is examining a painting with focused attention. To his left a young woman is studying him. And to his right another young man also studies him. The handsome man gradually realizes he is being stared at. Slowly he turns to his left and examines the woman and then turns to his right and examines the young man. He smiles slyly to the young man and moves on. The woman is left alone as the young man follows the handsome man.

☆☆☆

Laura is with a couple who have just bought a painting. Laura is placing a red dot on the corner of the wall card. The painting is a very erotic abstract flower painting—depicting what appears to be a floral vagina. The man is very pleased with the painting.

"I think you are going to be very happy with this," Laura adds. "A very wise investment. The artist had a sold-out show in San Francisco recently. And already her works have appreciated more than 200 percent in the past two years."

The wife seems less than convinced.

"Yes, an excellent investment," the husband agrees.

His wife uncertainly asks, "But where are we going to hang it?"

"How about over the fireplace?" her husband replies, all smiles.

"How about the laundry room," she suggests, with somewhat less enthusiasm.

☆☆☆

After the transaction is completed, Laura looks up when a young man in his twenties appears at the entrance. He is dressed casually and is darkly handsome and brooding. He surveys the room, sees Laura, and starts toward her.

"David, so you decided to join us after all." She looks at his clothes. "But you're not dressed."

He laughs. "I thought artists were exempt from monkey suits."

Laura glances nervously over at her husband who is still deeply engaged in conversation with the young woman.

"Well then, how about a drink?" She leads David toward the bar. "Oh, and I've got a possible sale of one of your paintings to the Eisenbergs. I'll let you know when it closes." She hands him a glass of champagne and then turns to leave.

He grabs her arm and turns her back toward him. "Don't treat me like this, please."

She avoids his gaze. "David..."

David reaches into his pocket. "Here, I have something for you." He hands her a small box. She stares at it. "Go ahead, open it."

"You're embarrassing me."

"How? You sell my work—I give you a little gift as a token of my...appreciation."

Laura turns away. "No."

David is suddenly very intense. "Why do you do this?"

"Because it's inappropriate."

"But you know how I feel about you," he insists.

192

She struggles for a reply. "No, David, I'm leaving." She turns, but he again grabs her arm and turns her back toward him.

"No, first you open the gift, and then *I'll* leave."

Laura looks around the gallery. Everyone seems occupied. "Very well." She heads to her office, and David follows her.

☆ ☆ ☆

Roland and Cash approach the *Touch Me* sculpture. Cash reaches out to touch it. Roland slaps his hand. "Don't you dare," he jokes. They laugh and move on, but as they leave, Cash reaches out behind Roland's back and, smiling, touches the sculpture. It begins to moan and rise.

☆ ☆ ☆

In Laura's office, she opens David's gift. Inside the box is a very beautiful, ceramic perfume bottle. It is very old, delicate, and obviously expensive. She is surprised and looks up at him.

"Why, this is exquisite. Egyptian? Twelfth dynasty?"

"Very good. Exactly. You like it?" he asks.

"Yes, but I can't accept this. It must have cost you a fortune."

"It's probably worth a painting or two."

She shakes her head, puts it back in the box, and holds it out for David to take back. "No, I can't."

But he doesn't take it. She can't resist and opens the bottle and takes in the fragrance. Her reaction is sudden and strange. "How did you know?"

"What?" he asks.

Laura smiles. "This is from your father, isn't it?"

David hesitates and then answers, "Not at all. I know your tastes."

"It's the perfume he always gave me."

David takes the bottle from her and smells its delicate fragrance. He looks at her. He touches his finger to the bottle and traces the perfume behind her ear and down the side of her neck and then down along the edge of her dress toward her breasts. She doesn't resist. In fact, she surrenders very softly. She doesn't speak, but looks David in the eyes.

193

Laura speaks softly. "Thank you."

David nods. "Now, as I promised, I shall go."

Laura reaches out to David. "How *is* your father?"

"Fine. He speaks of you often."

"Say hello to him for me, will you?"

He nods and then turns and leaves. She follows him out of the office. She watches as he leaves the gallery. She stands lost in thought. She closes her eyes, feeling the magical effect of the perfume. She traces along the line of her dress where he drew the line of perfume. She opens her eyes again and looks around the gallery. She notices things she did not see before. The sensuality of a black man's arm as he pours wine. A man's hand on the base of a woman's back. A woman whispering into the ear of her female partner. Mark leaning in close to the young woman. The lushness of the flowers. The rise and fall of a woman's breasts under sheer fabric.

"Can you tell me the price of that Brandise over there? Number eighty-three."

Suddenly Laura is forced back from her reverie. She turns toward a man holding a catalogue.

"I'm sorry..."

"Number eighty-three. The price?" he asks again.

Laura stands looking at him, unable to answer.

☆☆☆

All of the guests have gone. The caterers have taken down their tables, and are carrying out the last of their equipment. Laura stands at the front of the gallery, lost in thought. She watches Mark through the front window saying good-bye to the young woman, who then walks off down the street, glancing back at Mark before she disappears.

Randy comes up to Laura. "That's it, we're off."

She turns to Randy. "Thank you. It was perfect."

"Interesting crowd," he comments.

"Yes, wasn't it?"

"Shall I turn out the rest of the lights?"

She gathers her thoughts to respond with some difficulty. "Yes, please."

Randy turns out the lights and leaves. Laura sets the alarm, exits the gallery, and locks the door. The limo is parked at the curb. The driver hops out as Laura and Mark approach and opens the door for them. The car pulls away, and Laura and Mark sit in silence, lost in their own separate thoughts.

Mark sighs. "What a delightful evening."

As the car passes along the street, Laura sits back in her seat, discreetly tracing the places where David touched her with the perfume.

As the limo drives down the street, it comes to a stop sign. In a shop doorway, David steps out of the darkness and stares at Laura. She sees him, leans forward, and smiles as the limo starts up again.

"Yes, wasn't it?" she finally answers Mark, leaning back in her seat again. "A most successful opening."

David watches as the limo cruises down the street and disappears around a corner. He smiles and then turns, walking down the street and into the darkness.

Why You Must Brush Your Teeth

Sandra was running very late. And she had a very *big* and *important* early meeting this morning at her advertising agency. Crosby was putting the breakfast dishes in the dishwasher. Good boy.

"Busy day?" Crosby called from the kitchen.

Sandra was in the bedroom applying her lipstick in a mirror that had too much reflected light from the window, and she had to squint to get an even application.

"Frantic," she called back, as she checked the clock. *Oh my gosh.* She realized she needed to brush her teeth, but time was beating at her. She rushed toward the bathroom to brush, but just then Crosby appeared at the bedroom door, distracting her.

"What time will you be back?" he asked, as he picked up her purse and handed it to her.

"Ah, oh, let's see, I have the presentation this morning. Lunch with Corrine. Then having my hair done after work. About six, I would guess." She grabbed the purse from Crosby, picked up the portfolio with her Dooba Noodle presentation, gave Crosby a pat on the butt, and headed for the apartment door. She paused. "If you have a chance could you pick up the cleaning? They were closed when I went by yesterday."

"Sure...ticket?"

"Oh yeah." She slammed through her purse and pulled it out, handing it to him. "I really gotta go."

"Want me to make dinner? I was thinking spicy shrimp tacos."

It was so nice having a stay-at-home boyfriend. It almost made it worthwhile that he didn't have a job and brought absolutely no money into the house.

"That sounds terrific."

"Ah, and some money for the dry cleaning?" Crosby asked as he held out his hand.

She grabbed a twenty out of her purse, gave him a quickie kiss, and bounded out the door.

On the street, Sandra hailed a cab and settled into the back seat, and for the first time this morning, let out a sigh and relaxed. She pulled out a mirror from her bag to examine her appearance in preparation for the meeting—this very important meeting. She, as account executive, and her team had worked on this project for months—print, TV, and Internet marketing for a new Japanese food product. She had worked into the early morning putting the finishing touches on the presentation, now tucked safely away in her portfolio next to her on the seat of the cab.

She looked in the mirror and let out a subdued shriek. The taxi driver gave her a look. "You okay, lady?" he asked.

"Oh yes, I just forgot my contacts is all." She kept her lenses in the bathroom on the sink by her toothbrush so she would always remember to put them in after she brushed her teeth. She thought back to her disrupted morning and sighed once again. Did she have a spare pair at the office? She couldn't remember.

The cab pulled up at her office tower. She tried to focus on her wallet as she pulled out bills to pay the driver. She squinted, as she fumbled for her purse, and quickly exited the cab, as she was now running a bit late. She hoped the rest of her team was already there and keeping the clients happy. She dashed to the elevator and was halfway up to her office when she thought of one last refinement she wanted to add to one of the presentation boards. She looked down and, with a sharp pang, realized she had left her portfolio in the cab. She had completely missed the portfolio when she had scanned the seat before she got out. Damn forgetting her contacts.

She arrived at her floor, rushed to her office, and searched for another pair of contacts in her desk. She didn't have any. David, her assistant, appeared at the door.

"They're all waiting. Gordon is schmoozing with the clients and stalling. They need you to set up the presentation boards right away so they can get started. Mr. Davila is not a happy camper."

"Oh shit. David, can you call the team in here, please?"

He disappeared; and Sandra was frantic. She had no idea what to do. There were no duplicates of the work she had done overnight anywhere in the office. Everything was in that portfolio. All she could think to do was postpone the meeting and hope the cabbie would call when he found the portfolio. Fortunately, she had her business card inside.

The team was aghast when the situation was explained. Mr. Davila appeared at her office door, having learned of the disaster.

"What's this I hear?" One did not wish to hear that tone of voice.

"Yes, I'm s-o-o-o very sorry."

"Sorry doesn't cut it here, Sandra," Mr. Davila burned. He turned from the office door for a moment and then turned back and addressed the rest of her team. "Any of you have anything we can present?"

All shook their heads.

"Let me see if I can reschedule the clients. And Sandra, I want to see you in my office in five."

☆☆☆

Sandra was beyond despair while she waited for Corrine to show for lunch. She looked down at the two shopping bags filled with the belongings from her cleared-out office. She looked up and brushed away a few tears as Corrine came marching toward her. Corrine breezed into her chair, chipper as a cheerleader. She looked radiant in her simple black dress, setting off her chocolate skin tones.

"Girl, you look like one ton a mess. What up with you?" Corrine unfolded her napkin, spreading it across her lap like a blanket of snow.

Sandra plopped her head down on the tablecloth and groaned. She then explained the whole unearthly disaster.

"Uh huh," Corrine commented with just a touch of sass. "Well then we'd better have a bottle of tequila over here right now." She signaled for the waiter. "You got a plan, sweetie?"

Sandra, in a trance, stared at Corrine. "Well, I was thinking that if the cabbie calls, and we can retrieve the portfolio, and then Mr. Davila might reconsider. It really is a good presentation, and I think the client would go with it. Otherwise..." she gestured to the universe, suggesting the end of the world.

"Doll, I'm gonna clutch you up so bad. Pull yourself together. There's no way you're not gonna pull outta this—whatever happens. Come on now; let's have some oysters. The thought of them been dazzling me all morning. Uh huh."

Sandra began to calm down during lunch. Several tequilas and a Grand Marnier desert soufflé went a long way toward easing the shock. Sandra was very grateful for Corrine's soothing company and bright outlook and offered to pay for the lunch. She pulled out her credit card and insisted on taking the check.

The card came back declined. It was her company card, and they had already canceled it. She didn't have any other cards with her and not enough cash. Corrine stepped up and paid. Sandra was mortified.

"Don't worry about it, honey," Corrine comforted. "I should be taking you to lunch anyway, after the morning you've had. Why don't you just go home, and take a nice hot bath and a nap?"

"Oooh that sounds wonderful, but I have a hair appointment. Need a cut. Gotta look good when I hit the streets tomorrow job hunting."

"You'll be okay. I still think you might be able to work this out if you can find your portfolio. Did you notice the name of the cab company?"

"It was yellow is all I know."

"Yeah, that and about twenty million others. You need any money for the hairdresser's? I just went to the bank."

"No, I'm good. I have an account with them."

☆☆☆

Sandra arrived at the hairdresser's way before her appointment time. But they were able to squeeze her in early, even though they were always busy. She leaned her head back in the washbasin as Renaldo washed her hair. It felt so nice and warm, and she just let go and floated. The salon music was New Agey and tinkled. She almost fell asleep.

Renaldo roused her when he was done and led her to his station. She slumped into the chair. He helped her into the smock and prepared to start working on her.

"Do you need the roots tinted as well as the trim today?" he asked.

"Hum. Might be a good idea. Gotta look my very best."

"Okay, sweetie." He pulled out his hair color samples. "Do you remember which one we used last time?" He held the swatches up for her to examine. He could not check the color himself as her hair was wet and much darker now than when it was dry.

She squinted and peered at the tangle of samples. "Wasn't it that one?" She pointed to one.

"You sure?"

She nodded and then closed her eyes and retreated into the buzz of her inner turmoil as he blow-dried her hair before the tinting. Yes, a bath and a nap seemed very attractive to her at this moment. She actually fell asleep briefly as she waited for the tint to work its wonders. Renaldo awoke her, completed the rinse, and sent her to the dryers. Again, she let herself go and surrendered to the soft blowing breeze around her head.

When the drying was done, Renaldo led her back to the chair and began combing her out. He let out a gasp.

"What?" Sandra asked with stab of panic.

"I think we're going to have to redo the entire coloring. The roots don't match at all."

Sandra got out of the chair, walked up to the mirror, and squinted to see as best she could. There in the mirror was a zebra. The color was off by many shades. "Oh my God! Can you please fix it now?"

Renaldo went over to reception and checked the appointment book.

"I don't have a moment today. I can fit you in tomorrow at three. That's the best I can do."

"But what about the appointment I had at four today?" she pleaded.

"Oh hon, we've rescheduled that already. Your daddy is much in demand. I even have a waiting list. So on the mark, you know. But I can lend you a scarf. Three o'clock tomorrow is all I've got."

Sandra collapsed forward in the chair, fate pressing firmly on her shoulders. "Okay, give me the scarf," she sighed.

☆☆☆

Sandra emptied herself out of the cab. She'd had enough cash for the cab fare. The thought of her navigating the subway was way too much for her to bear today. She carefully checked the back seat this time and retrieved the bags of her office stuff. She was hoping there might be a call from the office with the glorious news that her portfolio had been found, with Mr. Davila pleading for her return.

She trudged her way to the elevator and up to her floor. She wearily unlocked the apartment door and let herself in. She closed the door behind her, leaned back against it, and closed her eyes. She was home. All would be well now. It was early, and she would have plenty of time for her bath and nap.

There was a wonderful aroma coming from the kitchen. She set down the bags and wandered to the kitchen. She checked the answering machine for messages. There were none. Perhaps Crosby had taken a message for her. She lifted the lid of the pot on the stove and took in the wonderful waft of sauce simmering away. Yes, she was beginning to feel better. And now, time for that bath and nap.

Where was Crosby? He was not in the living room, and she couldn't hear him at the computer. She wandered toward the bedroom and called out. "Crosby honey, you home?"

She heard a thump—the cat jumping down to greet her. She went to the bedroom and opened the door. There was a blur of activity, and without her contacts she could hardly focus. Almost before she knew it, a young man flashed by, pulling on a shirt as he swept out the apartment door. Crosby sat on the side of the rumpled bed. It was pretty hard to deny what had been going on. Sandra couldn't speak. She just stared at him.

"Well, now you know," Crosby finally said, without too much concern, as he stood and leisurely walked, stark naked, toward the bathroom. Just before going in he stopped and turned toward her and studied her a moment. "Nice scarf," he added and turned into the bathroom and closed the door.

☆☆☆

And that is why, boys and girls, we must always brush our teeth.

About the Author

Jon McDonald lives in Santa Fe, New Mexico. He has seven published novels, a memoir, and three children's books. His short stories have appeared in a number of prestigious publications. He considers himself a genre-bending author—he loves to take an established literary genre, play with it, and turn it on its head. He has lived abroad and traveled extensively.

Email: jonauthor@gmail.com
Website: www.jonmcdonaldauthor.com
Facebook: https://www.facebook.com/Jon-McDonald-146587072143639

Also by Jon McDonald

The Seed

NineStar Press, LLC

www.ninestarpress.com

www.ingramcontent.com/pod-product-compliance
Lightning Source LLC
Chambersburg PA
CBHW020322260626
47156CB00004B/1336